LANA

by
R.K. LILLEY

Candy,
XOXO
R.K. Lilley

Lana

ISBN-13: 978-0615822884
ISBN-10: 0615822886

Cover art by Warpuppy Art Studio

Interior design by Warkitty Formatting

www.rklilley.com

Give feedback on the book at:
authorrklilley@gmail.com

Twitter: @authorrklilley

Follow me on Instagram @authorrklilley

Like my page at www.facebook.com/RkLilley

Printed in the U.S.A

This book is dedicated to my husband, the love of my life, and my partner in crime, for always believing that writing was my path, even when I doubted it myself.

AN UP IN THE AIR NOVELLA

CHAPTER ONE

I felt overdressed the second I stepped off the plane. My simple white dress shirt, teamed with my tailored pale gray suit jacket, and its matching pale gray pencil skirt, had seemed wholly appropriate when I'd boarded the plane. But one second of breathing my beloved island air, and my outfit was all wrong. This was a business trip, so I hadn't even packed anything appropriate for the paradise of my childhood. I didn't even own anything like that anymore. The thought was demoralizing.

It wasn't even a particularly hot day. A cool breeze wafted across my skin as I stepped outside. I shrugged out of my blazer anyway, unbuttoning an almost indecent amount of buttons at the collar of my shirt. But cleavage didn't feel wrong here. I was now in a place where my typical wardrobe was usually a very tiny bikini. *Had I even packed one of those?*

I had resolved to set up meetings as soon as I arrived here, and so had dressed accordingly, but my resolve blew away with the gentle Maui breeze. I took deep breaths, loving the smell of the island air, which was divine, even mixed with jet fumes.

A car was already waiting for me at the curb, and a driver hustled out to take my sparse luggage. I towered over him in my red Jimmy Choo's. At five eleven, though, I would have towered over him even if I were wearing flats. "Ms. Middleton, how was your flight?" he asked.

I smiled at the familiar driver. He worked for my family's Maui resort. I quickly recalled his name. "I'm doing well, Thomas. How is island life these days?"

He flashed a grin at me. He was close to my own age of twenty-six, with a slight build and a quick smile. "Still can't tear myself away from this rock, so good. Bet you miss it." He gave me a sympathetic look. It was a look reserved for anyone crazy enough to leave this paradise behind for the mainland.

I sighed heavily. "You have no idea," I told him. My voice betrayed far more of my sorrow than I had intended. I mentally berated myself for being a downer at his crestfallen look.

He opened the car door for me, and I slipped in, sending him a reassuring look. "Sorry. I do miss it here, but it's not as bad as that."

He was behind the wheel before he asked, "To the hotel, Ms. Middleton?"

I started to say yes, but my heart took my mouth over suddenly. "To the Kalua shops."

He looked a little startled, but just nodded and started to drive.

The shops really weren't far from the hotel, I reassured myself. And I could pick up some island necessities for myself.

I rolled the window down as we drove. The wind quickly messed up my braid, and I pulled loose my wavy, streaky blonde hair in relief. It only hung to my mid-back now. When I had lived in paradise, it had hung all the way to my butt, with some streaks bleached nearly white by the sun. My skin was almost pale now, not sun-kissed, as I liked it. I'd had to grow up when I left paradise, and I looked it nowadays. Years off my beloved rock had taken their toll.

Thomas dropped me off at the Kalua shops with some reluctance. I waved him off, asking him to have my luggage taken to my room at the hotel. I reassured him that I would call him if I needed a ride. I knew that I wouldn't. One of the Kaluas would give me a ride; I was sure. They were my second family. I spoke to Tutu and Mari every week, in one form or another.

I had a death grip on my large handbag as I entered the surf shop. I wasn't brave enough to venture into the bar or the café just yet. I was still taking in the changes in the shop when I heard a shrill shriek from behind the counter. I was being hugged by a short, shapely woman in a flash. I hugged her back tightly, feeling unexpected tears prick my eyes. I felt instantly guilty that I had even considered going to the hotel first. Someone had been missing me, after all. I ran a hand down her thick black hair, affectionate with her in a way that I could never be even with my own mother.

"I didn't think you'd ever come back," she whispered, pulling back. Her eyes were a brown so dark they looked black. They were lovely and mysterious. *She* was lovely and mysterious. She was in her mid-forties now, but you wouldn't know it by looking at her. She was shapely, taking care of her body meticulously, and her face was a golden brown that time hadn't yet managed to so much as line. Her face was a lovely combination of her mixed Japanese-Hawaiian heritage. Her lips were full, her nose small and pert, her eyes large and almond shaped. She was petite, but by no means slight. Not one part of her was thin, nor was it fat. She was just…shapely, down to her perfect ankles. She wore a half-shirt, and tiny shorts, just like I remembered, and she still worked them better than any twenty-year old I'd ever met. She wore a white plumeria in her hair, as ever.

"We talk every week, Auntie. You can hardly say I don't keep in touch."

She just smiled at me, but it was a sad smile. "I know, but it's not the same. When are you coming back home, Lana?"

I bit my lip, feeling strangely adrift at the question. This *was* home, but I couldn't come back. It hurt to even think about it. "Well, I'm here for now. I came for business, but I realized that I didn't bring anything appropriate outside of work clothes."

She just smiled, eyeing me up. "Well, you do look kind of hot in that, but yeah, you need to get your island back on. Go say hi to Tutu. I've got you covered, pretty girl."

I gave her a grateful smile, moving to the door that joined Tutu's café with the surf shop. Mari stopped me with a word. She rushed to me, putting a plumeria in my hair, just over my ear. I fingered it, smiling.

She sighed, as though in great relief, and fingered the identical flower over her own ear. "Much better. Go on."

I stopped at the door, a sudden thought stopping me. "Is Akira…?"

She just gave me wide eyes. "Last I heard, he was off at some business meeting."

I sighed in relief. I just wasn't prepared to see him yet. I nodded and opened the door.

Tutu gave me the same treatment, shrieking like a crazy woman and running to me like she was far younger than her years. She had to be in her sixties by now, I knew.

I hugged her back tightly. She was a tiny woman, her Japanese heritage showing much more strongly in her than her Hawaiian half, both in her body and face. She had pale skin, and pitch-black hair. I fingered it, and we touched the flowers in each other's hair with warm smiles.

"You're home," she breathed.

I took a deep breath, because for some strange reason, I wanted to cry. I was brought out of my moment of weakness by a series of framed photos on the wall of the café. It was set up as a sort of collage of magazine covers and editorial pictures. I laughed at the thoroughness of it. My short, unimpressive modeling career was pretty well represented on that large expanse of wall. Tutu followed my gaze, smiling proudly. "I tell everyone about how you grew up here."

I shook my head, a little embarrassed. Modeling was something I'd often said I'd never do as a young teen. My mother had been an iconic model of the eighties, and I'd known that, although I took after her looks strongly, I could never match her career. And I hadn't. The worst part of it was, as short as my modeling career had been, I'd still suspected that every job I ever got was because of who my mother was, and not anything to do with my modeling 'talent'.

But the pictures on the wall did look nice enough, I supposed. Some of them were high fashion, but even more were bikini shots. I had been a skinny kid, but gotten very voluptuous around the time I'd also gotten awkwardly tall. It made me much more suited to swimsuit modeling, I had quickly found. A lot of designers absolutely despised boobs.

I had only modeled for one memorable year when I was just eighteen, before settling down to get a business degree, and then to work for the family business of owning and running a worldwide hotel chain. But I still got sighted by strangers from the modeling. I supposed I should have been flattered and not so embarrassed about the whole thing. I had apparently left some kind of impression.

"Akira has become well-known for threatening anyone who says anything the slightest bit dirty about those bikini pictures. He threw a fit, at first, when I put them up, but I stood firm. I'm proud of my Lana, I told him. Her unmatched modeling career will not be forgotten by me, I told him!"

I had to laugh at her description of my short career. Even *I* didn't dare argue with her about defending me, though. She was a formidable, if tiny, woman. I stroked her hair affectionately. She still hadn't let go of me, and I didn't mind.

I stiffened as a familiar figure strode through the doors that adjoined the bar to the café. Tutu patted my back, but finally relinquished her impressively firm hold on me, moving to the woman who had just entered. "What do you need?" she asked the other woman. It was downright rude, for Tutu.

Milena didn't answer her. Her shocked gaze was glued to mine. She was a tall woman, a few inches shorter than me, but still tall. She had a trim, toned figure, with large, gravity defying breasts that were shown off to perfection in an island half shirt, 'Kalua's Bar' stretched tight over that ample chest. Her skin was golden and perfect everywhere. She had a mixed heritage as well, though I didn't know the exact mix. But her genetics were stellar, wherever their origins. Her face was pretty, her pouty mouth positively sinful. I had always wanted to be her. She had everything I wanted. I hated her, as I always had.

I nodded at her politely. "Milena. Long time, no see." It was the most civil thing I could manage to say to her.

She just huffed, not even trying to return the civility. I really didn't care. I hated her so much that I would have been a little stung if she didn't hate me back, at least a little. She didn't even stay to get whatever she had come for, just leaving with a whispered, "haole," under her breath.

piece suit, and I couldn't help it, I eyed him top to bottom, taking in every delectable detail of his tall, muscular length. He was a shrewd businessman at heart, but he had the look of a heavyweight boxer or a fit pro-wrestler, with his massive size. And I knew it was all muscle under his clothes. There wasn't an ounce of fat on his perfect body.

I was proud to see that I recovered more swiftly than he did at our chance meeting. He still just stared at me, total shock showing on his hard face. I bent down, and began to pick up my scattered bag of goodies.

"Lana?" he spoke finally, his voice hoarse.

I straightened, smiling at him. It was my best, falsely bright smile. "Akira."

His arms raised, as though to embrace me, but dropped, probably at the shocked look on my face. I hadn't expected him to ever want to touch me again, for any reason.

Impulsively, I walked to him, throwing my arms around his neck for a hug. He wrapped strong arms around me instantly, and I closed my eyes, burrowing into his chest as though I were still a child. This felt like home. Home was a lie, I knew. But I let myself live the lie, for a few minutes, at least. I breathed him in. He smelled divine, like the ocean, and the island, and himself. The best smell in the world. I felt him stroking my hair, his cheek pressed to the top of my head. I don't think either of us had a clue what to say, so we stood like that for long minutes, just comforting each other.

"How are you?" he finally asked. Mortifyingly, the question brought tears to my eyes. *Adrift*, I thought. *I'm just adrift, banned from my home, and utterly rejected by the only man I'll ever love.* I wanted to hate him for it, but I just couldn't. I had only ever known how to love him. Whole-heartedly. Too much so.

I swallowed hard, finally answering the innocent question. "Busy. Busy with work, as usual. How are you?" I finally pulled out of his arms, my tears mercifully dried.

I looked up into his eyes. They were troubled.

"The same, I guess. All of the businesses are prospering, so things are good. I didn't know you were in town. How long have you been here?"

"I got in this afternoon. I just finished visiting with Tutu and Auntie." As I spoke, Akira bent down, gathering up my things. I blushed when he handled some rogue lingerie. It was a tiny scrap of nothing that had nothing to do with island wear. I had no idea why Mari had added it to the bag. He paused when he saw it, then hurriedly shoved it into the bag. I didn't bend down to help him, strangely transfixed as he handled several of my new, tiny bikinis. It made my face flush, and my skin heat. His hands were so big, and the bikinis were so tiny. And I remembered those hands. Those wonderful, talented, perfect hands...

"It looks like you're planning a trip to the beach." He grinned up at me. "Let me know if you want company. We could go to the old spot and try to catch some waves."

I agreed before I could wise up and turn him down. "Okay."

He straightened, handing me my purse, but carrying the over-stuffed bag for me. "We could go right now, if you're up for it. I just finished up for the day."

I knew I should say no, to preserve a little of my sanity, but I just couldn't do it. "Sounds great. I just need to change into one of those bikinis."

He was eyeing the keys in my hand, his brow furrowed.

"Auntie loaned me her car. I was going to have one of the hotel drivers bring it back for me," I explained.

He led me to a dark SUV instead, opening the passenger door for me, and putting my bag in the back. He turned on the car, cool air rushing out of the A/C vents immediately. I sat in the seat, and he came back to my door, crowding me a little. "I'll go return her keys, since I can drive you." He touched the flower in my hair lightly, his eyes intense. "Be right back."

He was gone for maybe a minute before I realized that I could just change while he was gone. I had changed into my swimsuit in his car countless times. Why should it be any different now? I climbed into the back seat, sliding out of my stilettos and then my tight skirt. I grabbed the first matching bikini pieces that I saw, slipping on the bottom before taking off my top. Because I was trying to hurry, my fingers fumbled with every button of my blouse.

I unsnapped my front-clasping bra, shrugging out of it. I realized, only after I was topless, that the bikini top was a tangled mess. I was still untangling the thing when Akira opened the driver's seat door.

He froze, just froze, staring at my naked breasts. They were heaving in agitation, my nipples hard from the car's blasting A/C.

I grimaced at him. "Sorry. I thought I'd save us a trip and get my swimsuit on now," I said, expecting him to close his door and wait outside, to give me privacy. The windows were tinted dark enough that they did actually conceal most of the interior of the car.

But he didn't close the door. Instead, he sat, buckling his seat belt. And then he did something that absolutely stunned me. He reached up one of his big, dark hands, and adjusted his rearview mirror, blatantly watching me. It froze me in my tracks, and I was too surprised to move for long moments, my breasts quivering as my breaths grew jerky and uneven.

Finally, I bent back down to the stubborn bikini top, working on untangling the strings. But I couldn't focus on the task for more than a few seconds, my eyes flying back to Akira's as he watched me in the mirror, his heavy-lidded eyes very obviously on my breasts. I arched my back, showing them off to better advantage. I had been a professional poser at one time, I told myself, so why not use it to my benefit?

His jaw went a little slack, and I felt myself growing wet. To affect him like that, to make him want me, was the biggest turn on in the world to me. I had been kneeling on the seat to change, but I shifted my position, facing him, on my knees now on the seat. I leaned back, letting my arms rest along the seat, the movement thrusting my breasts forward provocatively. He sucked in a harsh breath, but didn't look away, didn't speak. I cupped both of my breasts in my hands, kneading them. They overflowed in my hands, and I pushed them together, stroking them up until my nipples just peeked out between my fingers. I pinched them, and Akira's head fell back against his headrest, his breathing audibly heavy now. Still, we didn't speak. And he never took his eyes off me.

I further surprised the both of us when I ran one hand lower, down my taut stomach, and between my legs. I parted my knees on the seat, giving him a perfect view as I plunged a hand into my bikini bottoms and fingered myself.

"Untie them," Akira said, his voice sounding rusty. "Please. I want to see what your fingers are doing."

I pulled the little bows on each side of the string bikini, baring myself with a few simple motions. He groaned, and that made me weak. To affect *him* like that. It was all I had ever wanted. I ran my fingers over my sex, showing myself to him very clearly. I stroked my clitoris, then thrust a finger inside of my sex.

Abruptly, he closed his eyes, cursing. "I'm so sorry, Lana. Please, just get dressed. I was out of line. I'm sorry."

And just like that, all of my hopes were dashed, and I just felt dirty and ugly, and inevitably, unwanted. I grabbed a different bikini, this one skin-toned, but not tangled. I put it on hurriedly, stepping out of the car, and into the front seat. I couldn't even look at him. "I'm dressed. Are we still going to the beach, or would you prefer to just drop me off?" I asked, my voice weak.

I knew Akira had finally opened his eyes because he suddenly began to curse. "Jesus, Lana, you look naked in that suit. That thing is indecent."

I glanced down at it, surprised by his words. The bikini was scant and skin-colored, but hardly indecent. I realized that he probably just didn't want to see so much of my skin, especially after my sordid little peep show. He'd obviously seen enough. I felt my lip quiver at the realization. "Sorry. I'll put a shirt on, and you can just drop me off at the hotel," I said in the most even tone I could manage, opening the door to get my things.

He stopped me by grabbing my wrist in his hard grip, pulling me back into the car.

CHAPTER THREE

"I'm sorry. That came out all wrong. The suit is fine. Let's just go to the beach, k?" His voice was oh so gentle, and I realized that he must have seen my lip quiver at his rejection.

I looked firmly out the window. I doubted I could ever look him in the eye again. "You don't have to," I said. I knew I sounded like a sullen child.

He made a little noise of sympathy in his throat, stroking my hair. "Oh, Lana," he whispered. "I only ever seem to hurt you, no matter what I do. I want to take you to the beach. So let's go, k?"

He spoke to me like I was a child with fragile feelings, and I was so pathetic that I soaked it up, knowing very acutely that even scraps were better than nothing. "K."

He patted the top of my head. It was a 'good girl' pat, but I didn't protest. "Do you mind if I stop by my place to change real quick? I don't have anything in the car, if you can believe it. Oh, and we need surfboards, of course."

"Oh, yeah, surfboards," I said absently, just looking out the window, trying to keep my mind blank so I wouldn't do something stupid, like cry in front of him.

The house he pulled up to was drastically different from the last time I had seen it. It looked like it was a completely different house now, all modern architecture and sleek, reflective windows. And it was noticeably bigger. "You expanded, huh?"

I felt him studying me, but I still didn't look at him. "Yes. I've made quite a few changes, over the years. Come on in." He got out of the car as he spoke, coming around to my side and opening my door. I got out, looking at anything but him. He gripped my arm just above the elbow, pulling me firmly to his front door, then ushering me in. "I'll be quick. Make yourself at home," he said, stroking a hand down my hair, then disappearing up the stairs.

I walked through the main floor slowly, taking in all of the changes rather numbly. It had turned from a somewhat rundown beach house into an ultra-modern, sunlit infused haven. The color scheme was simple, with lots of white and pale gray and a few touches of bright color. A bright yellow vase on the mantle, and a colorful painting in the living area, just splashes of color here and there, all of the neutral bringing that color out more vividly. The whole space was open now, with only glass walls. But the windows were the most spectacular change, lining the walls now, letting in the light, for clear, clean views of the beach. Apparently, business had been good for Akira. I was glad.

Akira changed quickly, joining me near the window as I gazed at the ocean. He walked up behind me, and I still didn't look at him.

He tugged on a lock of my hair gently. "Hey. Will you at least look at me?"

I finally did, and was immediately sorry. He wore only a pair of black board shorts, of course. I could see the many thick black tattoos that dotted the front of his muscular shoulders. The tribal patterns traced down to his mid back, I knew. I loved those tattoos. His abs were as washboard hard as ever. I tried not to drool as I took in his perfect naked torso. I finally tore my eyes away from his golden skin to look into his troubled gaze. "Your house looks amazing," I told him.

He just nodded, studying my face. "I've upset you. How can I make it better?" he asked, his voice so serious and quiet.

I felt my face crumple, and he enfolded me in his arms. I buried my face in his chest, in the spot right between his muscular pectorals. I pressed my body full against him, wanting to stay wrapped in those arms forever. This was why I could never come back here. My feelings hadn't dimmed with time; they'd merely been pushed back into a dark corner of my heart, ignored, as I was deprived of his intoxicating presence. But to him, to him, I was only a burden. *A family friend with an inconvenient infatuation*, I recalled, was how he'd phrased it. Those had been his words to Milena at the time. And that had been the day after I'd seduced him.

"I don't know what's wrong with me," I said against his chest, not willing to pull away, even to speak.

He made that sympathetic little humming noise in his throat, kissing the top of my head softly. "It's me. I'm a bastard. I'm sorry. And you're probably tired from the flight. Wanna take a nap? We can try the beach later, or even on another day."

I made a sound of protest. "I leave in two days."

I felt his chest expand on a deep breath. "Wow. I was hoping you'd stay a bit longer. That's so short, after all of those years away. Don't you miss it here, just a little?"

I wanted to sob like a baby. I wanted to hit him. It was such a cruel question, coming from him. But I just stayed flush against him as tears ran down my cheeks in an embarrassing flood.

His chest rumbled in distress as he felt my tears streaming down my face and then his chest. "Oh, baby, how you must hate me."

I sobbed at that, because I didn't. Because I couldn't.

He picked me up, cradling me like the baby I was. He kissed my forehead as he carried me upstairs. My eyes were closed when he laid me on his bed. I wouldn't let go of him when he tried to straighten. He laughed, a sweet little rumble against my cheek. "Is there a reason that you're hanging onto me like a monkey?" he asked, amused.

"Can you stay with me, for just a minute?"

He made a soothing sound as he lay down beside me. I tried to cuddle closer, but saw that he'd put a pillow between our lower regions. I shrank back, my shoulders hunched. He was wary even to touch me. And he should have been. I was an infatuated fool, just like he'd said. I turned away from him, burying my face in his pillow. It smelled like him; I wanted to take it home. He threw an arm around me from behind, pulling my back against his chest, and my butt against the... pillow. He spoke against my ear. "We all missed you, you know. It hasn't been the same without you. Not even close."

"I thought you hated me," I said quietly, holding my breath to hear his answer.

He cursed, but stroked my hair, as though to soften the cursing. "Never, Lana. *Never.* I was afraid of that. Am I the reason you've stayed away for so long?"

I didn't answer, and he squeezed me tighter. "You're right, I just need a nap. I'm out of my mind tired. I'm not usually like this, I swear."

He sighed against me. "You take a nap. I'll make us some dinner, k?"

I didn't answer, just burrowed more deeply into his divinely smelling bed.

He kissed the top of my head before leaving me. He didn't hate me, I thought, as I drifted off to sleep. It was something.

I was wrapped in Akira's arms again when I awoke. There was no pillow now. My leg was hiked up high on his hip, our chests rubbing together with every breath. I glanced at his face. Still asleep. I moved against him very slightly, and found that not *all* of him was asleep. I moved again, and moaned. His erection was so hard and thick, straining at his shorts in a glorious display. I knew he was only responding to me because he was asleep, but it didn't seem to matter. I began to rub against him, panting as our chests rubbed together, and his hard cock rubbed against my sex. His hand caressed my hip, pulling me closer as he grunted in his sleep, eyes still closed.

My tiny bikini suddenly felt so oppressive, and I untied the top impatiently, rubbing my nipples against his chest. The hand on my hip moved up, kneading at the pliant flesh. I turned onto my back to give him better access. He stroked my full, sensitive breasts until I squirmed. I untied my bikini bottoms, guiding his hand lower, putting his fingers right on my sex. His talented fingers took over from there, rubbing and stroking until I was panting.

I glanced at his face. His eyes were still closed, but his face was flushed, his breath harsh. "Mmm, Lana," he murmured, his fingers plunging inside of me. His erection was pressed against my hip now, and I touched him, stroking him roughly over his shorts. "Milena," he said, his voice sounding irritated. But still, the sound of her name on his lips froze me in my tracks. I tugged his busy hand out of me, extricating myself from him with regret. He didn't know what he was doing, and I had very nearly taken advantage of that fact. I curled into a ball, shrinking away from him. I felt him wake with a start a moment later. He hugged me from behind again, as though nothing had happened, and began to relax back into sleep.

He felt along my hip, and then, very lightly, felt the spot on my back, where my bikini should be tied. He cursed, and I felt him begin to search for the missing scraps of material. I rolled onto my back, throwing an arm over my eyes. He sucked in a breath as he looked at me. He shook my shoulder lightly. I parted my legs slightly, arching my back a little to give him a better view, my arm still covering my eyes stubbornly.

I felt him freeze, and I knew that he was staring at me. He didn't move for so long that I shifted again, parting my legs farther apart, wanting to see what he would do. *Could he see how wet I was?* The room was far from dark. From the light streaming in the window, I would have guessed that it was late afternoon.

I felt Akira move off the bed, and heard the sound of rustling clothing, then the unmistakable sound of flesh slapping against flesh.

He would rather jerk himself off than touch me, I thought, shocked and furious at the thought.

I lifted my arm from my eyes, unable to keep from looking. He was standing at the edge of the bed, gloriously naked, and gripping his huge erection in both hands. His jaw was clenched, his nostrils flared. He released himself as our eyes met, swallowing hard. "I'm sorry," he said quietly. It was his favorite phrase lately. I hated it.

I ran my hands down my body, and his eyes followed them hungrily. "Is it really so hard for you to touch me?" I asked him quietly.

He sighed, moving closer to me slowly, as though afraid to scare me. "You were asleep, and naked. I must have stripped you in your sleep. That was so out of line of me, I kno—" His sentence broke off as I began to touch my sex, angling my body to give him a hell of a view. His fists clenched, but he crawled a little closer, watching my hands work.

"Do you think you might have a vibrator, or maybe even a cock, that I could borrow?" I asked him archly when he just continued to watch me.

His eyes flew to mine, and they were almost panicked. "Are you sure? I don't want to take advantage of you. Again."

I wanted to scream, he was so exasperating. "I was eighteen, Akira, fully legal. Quit acting like you were a predator. I seduced you, if you recall."

He gave me a stern look. "I'm ten years older, and you were barely legal, and a virgin. And your father trusted me to look after you, not to violate you. It was a bastard thing to do."

I writhed on the bed, stroking myself shamelessly when I spoke. "I'm twenty-six now. Can we get over it already?"

I wanted him to crawl on top of me and bury himself deep, fucking me hard enough to make me forget that it was a pity fuck. He didn't do that. Instead, he grabbed my hand, bringing my wet fingers to his mouth, and sucking them clean. My jaw went slack. It was the sexiest thing I'd ever seen in my life, his eyes closing in pleasure as he tasted me. He released my limp hand, then gripped my legs open, and buried his face there. He began to suck and lick and stroke, working me hard with his tongue and teeth before he started on me with thick fingers. A sound tore from my throat, my fingers and hands rubbing again and again over his thick hair. I clutched him to me, saying his name, again and again, as he brought me to climax.

CHAPTER FOUR

He perched his chin on my stomach, just above my pelvic bone, watching me come back down from the blissful orgasm. His eyes were gentle as he studied me. "I could do that to you all day. Again?"

I fought the sudden childish urge to yank his hair out. "I'm on the pill, and I'm quite clean. Are you so repelled at the thought of just fucking me?" I asked him, deliberately crude and goading. It was a new tactic, so maybe it would work.

He rose onto his elbows, giving me that stern, older brother look that he was so fond of. But he was still hard and quivering as he knelt on his knees between my open thighs. He opened my legs wider as he knelt there, staring down at me. "I just want to be sure that this is what you want. I don't want to take ad—"

I interrupted that infuriating phrase of his by sitting up, gripping his hard cock in my hand. I stroked him hard, rolling until I could kneel down far enough to take him in my mouth. I sucked on him desperately, as though my life depended on it.

He tried to pull me away by the hair, but I was determined. He was moaning roughly, calling my name rather urgently, but I just kept stroking him firmly with my hand and working on him with my mouth.

"Baby, get on your back. I'm going to fuck you. Get on your fucking back," he nearly shouted.

It got my attention, and I fell back.

He followed me down, pinning me roughly and thrusting into me with one smooth motion. I wanted to cry, it felt so good. He began to move, his strokes long and slow. His dark eyes looked into mine with an intensity that I couldn't ignore. "You have the most amazing eyes in the world, Lana. I think I've missed those eyes the most." My eyes were a deep blue that, depending on the lighting, looked almost violet. "You were this perfect, enchantingly beautiful girl that made the world brighter just by being in it, and you were ours. I can't tell you how sorry I am that I drove you away." As he finished speaking, he bent down to kiss me, his strokes getting faster, and harder. I moaned into his mouth, and he stroked a tongue into mine. I gave it a little bite, and he groaned, one of his hands pulling my thighs higher, and wider, and ramming into me, harder and harder. He pulled his mouth free, watching me intently as he snaked a hand down my body, rubbing my clit as he rode me. I came, and he followed me, shouting my name, every muscle in his body straining as he buried himself to the hilt, rubbing his orgasm out inside of me with sexy little thrusts that went on and on.

He rolled onto his back, throwing an arm over his eyes when he'd recovered. "Fuck," he cursed.

I sat up, worried. *Did he regret it, already? Couldn't I at least get one night of pleasure before it all came crashing down again?*

I stood and walked, naked, to the window. It was huge, with a perfect view of the ocean. I leaned my head against it.

"You are gonna give some lucky bastards quite the show if you plaster your body to the window like that."

I glanced back at him, pressing a breast very deliberately against the glass. "Oops," I said, batting my eyelashes at him in a mock innocent pose. The beach was empty at the moment, so I wasn't worried about it.

He gave me an exasperated look. "You are as sassy as ever. Some things never change."

I arched my back, wiggling my bum at him, just a little bit. "Do you need to spank me?"

I watched, in frozen fascination, as his semi-hard cock came to full attention again. He groaned, as though it were the most bothersome thing in the world.

It wasn't bothersome to me.

I leaned against the window, arching my back and parting my legs. I lay my cheek against the glass as I sent him what I hoped was a sultry look. "We already had sex. Why stop at once? The damage is done, right?"

He was striding to me before I'd finished taunting him. He grabbed my hips from behind, pressing hard against me, and working himself in, inch by hard inch. He went slowly at first, making sure that I could take all of him at that angle. After he'd cleared my passage twice, he began a pounding rhythm that had me making desperate little sounds in my throat. My climax built fast. He grabbed my breasts, squeezing and kneading at them. "I've jerked myself off to your pictures more times than I can count," he whispered into my ear.

That did it. I came, gasping out his name.

He jerked into me a half a dozen more times before he reached his own climax, clutching at my breasts and biting my neck almost roughly. I loved the rawness of it.

He pulled me into bed with him after that, cuddling against me. I hadn't forgotten how sweet he could be. The memories still haunted me. Often.

"Did you really masturbate to my pictures, or were you just saying that?" I asked him, looking up to see his eyes.

He looked down at me, where I cuddled in my little spot on his chest, his expression baffled. "Why the hell would I just say that? It's perverted and nasty, not to mention embarrassing. I felt like I needed to get it off my chest. And it's not 'did', it's 'do'. When I jerk off to a picture, I guarantee it's yours."

I laughed, loving the disgruntled look on his face. "Prove it. I haven't modeled in years. Where would you even get my picture?"

He gave me a pointed look, pushing me gently from his chest. He rolled to the side of the bed, reaching underneath it to pull out a rather beat-up issue of Sports Illustrated. Sure enough, I was on the cover. "Exhibit A," he muttered. It was the most high profile modeling job I'd ever done, my fifteen minutes of fame, posing in a tiny yellow bikini and straddling a surfboard on the coveted cover spot. I'd walked away from the business after that job, feeling a strange but overwhelming need, at the time, to reconnect with my family, and the family business. Modeling just hadn't been for me, and I'd burned out on it quickly.

I smiled at Akira. "You know I don't mind. You can use my pictures in any filthy way you want to, you pervert."

He flushed, and I laughed. I enjoyed tormenting him. I always had. For years and years, it had been my favorite hobby.

"It drives me crazy sometimes, thinking about how many other men are doing exactly the same thing."

I just shrugged, not really concerned about anyone else so much as *him*. He had always been the only one I cared about, the only one I saw or concerned myself with. It was the joke of my pathetic life that he didn't feel even remotely the same way about me.

"What else? Is there an exhibit B? What other pictures do you have of me that you like to do filthy things to?" I asked.

He glared, but walked to his computer. "Observe. Exhibit B. See my browsing history?" He clicked on it, and another bikini shot of me popped up. This one was more scandalous. It had been taken when I was surfing, some discarded shot from a photo shoot, maybe. But someone had leaked it. I was straddling the surfboard, looking intently at the waves, one of my nipples showing clearly due to a wardrobe malfunction.

I laughed. I hadn't even known that was out there. "I've never seen that one."

"I made the mistake of reading the comments under it once. It was the angriest jerk-off session of my life."

I laughed, feeling positively giddy at the thought of him wanting me that much, enough to search me online to see a picture of me.

We were both still naked. Neither of us had even thought to cover up as we looked at the computer. He sat in his computer chair, just staring at me, dumbstruck. His gaze ran up and down my body hungrily, but he was still so hesitant to touch me. My hands skimmed along my naked torso. "Which do you prefer, the photo-shopped pictures, or the real thing?" I asked, cupping my breasts as I finished.

He swallowed hard, looking up into my eyes. "It's like you have no clue how far out of my league you are. Guys like me don't get girls like you. You know that, right? You're a filthy rich supermodel, who also happens to be the daughter of my mentor, the man I respect more than anyone else in the world. I've never even met my own father; I've had my share of run-ins with the law, on several occasions, in fact, when I was a stupid, violent teenager. I still struggle to keep my fists to myself with the wrong provocation. I almost punched a guy in the bar just last week for talking about those damned pictures my mom won't take down. I'm not *good enough* for you."

I just listened to him as he dissed himself, wanting to *punch* him, but wanting to hear where he was going with his tirade even more.

I sat on his lap, or rather, I straddled him, naked. It was a mistake. He closed up like a clam after that, looking at my body, his eyes so hungry and tender.

It undid me, such a harsh looking man with such tender eyes for me. When I was certain he didn't have any more to say, I leaned in and began to kiss him, a hungry, passionate kiss. I wrapped my arms around his neck, rubbing against him like a cat. I assumed he couldn't go for another round, but I just wanted that raw, naked contact with him. I was more than delighted when I felt him growing hard again against me. I shifted against him, instinctively trying to impale myself on the stiffening length.

He pulled back with a rough groan. "I'm not fucking you again until I've at least fed you. I'll feel like a complete jerk if you pass out from hunger."

"After," I murmured, rubbing against him.

He let me, watching me as though mesmerized.

"Just pretend I'm a picture of me, and that my vagina is your hand."

He spanked my ass hard for that one. He even threw me over his shoulder, standing and striding from the room as he did so. I loved that he was so big that it was no effort for him to carry me around like that. "Fine, fine," I said between giggles. "My mouth can be your hand."

He swatted me several more times as he carried me down the stairs. He tossed me onto his soft, white leather sofa, and I saw that he was grinning. That smile was all it took to flood me with the years of memories that had made me fall so helplessly for him.

Memories of this hard, mean-looking man who didn't have a soft bone in his hard-muscled body, but who could always muster up the softest, sweetest smile, reserved just for me. I had been a willful, spoiled, stubborn child, dogging his every step, insisting that he take me to the beach during his precious free time.

He had patiently taught me to surf, spending countless hours in the ocean with me as I learned. It had been a slow process. I hadn't been a quick learner at all, but I had been determined. And if anyone so much as looked wrong at the little white girl who couldn't surf for shit, but still took up a precious spot at one of the best surf spots, Akira was more than happy to set them straight. He had been scary when he got protective. He was always ready for a fight. But I had never been scared. I had adored that he was only a softy for *me*. No one else could make his eyes go soft like I could, and I had been paying attention.

Even his long-time, on-again off-again girlfriend didn't get the tender looks that he bestowed on me. And when I would finally catch on, picking up whatever thing I got into my head *that* week for him to teach me, he would pat me on the head, give me that smile that I craved, and say softly, "Good job, Lana. I'm so proud of you."

My mind swung back to the present when he spoke, walking into his kitchen.

"It's nice to have the old, infuriating Lana back. I missed my little giggling vixen. Don't move. We can eat right here."

I scrambled up, disregarding his order completely. "Um, eat on a white sofa? Are you crazy? And I'm filthy. You really shouldn't set me on anything clean right now." I followed him into the kitchen, pressing against his back as he dug through the fridge. "I'm so full of your cum right now that it's dripping down my leg," I whispered in his ear, wanting to get a reaction. I got one.

He had me on my back on his table between one breath and the next. He was spreading my legs, studying me for evidence of what I'd said. It was there. "One more time," he told me, his voice a sexy rasp. "Then we eat, and shower."

"Yes," I gasped. He put my ankles on his shoulders and plunged in with a groan, working in and out of me very slowly at first, testing my soreness with a few concerned questions. He was rubbing my clit as he asked them, and I sent him a passion-infused glare. "I'm fine," I told him, and he thrust much harder. "More than fine. I'm getting my brains fucked out by the hottest man on the planet."

He liked that assessment, his breath getting faster, his thrusts harder and heavier as he got closer to his climax. He rubbed a finger on my clit almost frantically, trying to catch me up to him.

I was there the whole time, coming when he did, watching his warm brown eyes the entire time.

He didn't move after we'd finished, just stayed buried deep, smiling down at me. He stroked a hand along my torso, caressing softly.

"You feel so good, Lana. Fuck, you're as tight as you were when I took your virginity. Fucking unbelievable."

"You're just so big, I'm not sure you could tell the difference," I told him. He squeezed my breast hard for that one. "I love having you inside of me, love your hands on me. You jerk off to my picture? I get off to the memory of our first time together."

"Well, well, well, isn't that cute?" Milena drawled from the open front door. No other voice in the world could have been more unwelcome in that moment.

CHAPTER FIVE

W^e were clearly visible from her vantage point, in about the most vulnerable position imaginable. She glared at Akira, but when she swung her hate-filled eyes to me, I knew that I was the real object of her fury.

"I always knew it," she screeched. "You lying asshole! I always knew that you'd slept with her." She pointed a finger at me. "I'm going to mess up your face, you stupid whore. I'm going to put your skinny ass in the hospital for this."

Akira had to slip out of me noisily to walk to the deranged woman. "You need to calm the fuck down, Milena. Lana, please get dressed and wait outside. Your clothes are by the door."

I did as he said, the entire situation suddenly coming into focus for me. I grabbed the first island dress I saw, shrugging into it, grabbed my handbag, and rushed out the front door. I didn't wait outside, though. I just started walking, in no direction in particular, my mind racing.

Oh, god, are those two still together? I felt ill at the thought.

But he'd gone to comfort her and just kicked me out, like I was trash. Or the other woman, whom his girlfriend had just caught him fucking.

I barely made it to some nearby bushes before I emptied out the contents of my stomach, the thought made me so sick.

I had just assumed, because the engagement had been called off, that they weren't together anymore. But she apparently had a key to his house, and he'd so obviously been distressed that she'd found us together. I'd seen his face. It had been downright panicked as he'd told me to wait outside.

I wandered off the small road, walking rather aimlessly, pointed towards the beach.

How many times and how many ways, could my heart be broken by that man?

He just didn't feel for me the way I felt for him, and he never would. It didn't work that way, I knew.

I had tried to be interested in other men after I'd left for the mainland. In college, and even in my short modeling career, I had dated, even tried to hook up, but I wasn't interested in other men. It just wasn't in me to love or even want anyone that wasn't Akira. I couldn't force myself to have those kinds of feelings, just like he couldn't force himself to love me the way I longed for. It was a hard lesson that I'd thought I'd learned years ago.

Yet here I was again, heartbroken as though I'd let myself hope again for his unattainable love. And there was always Milena, somewhere in the picture. She must be the one that he adored, the only one he could really see. I could understand that kind of devotion, but that didn't make it hurt any less. It hurt more, to be the seductress who had tempted him so shamelessly from the one he obviously loved. I hated that the most, that I might be the other woman. I didn't want to be that, not ever, not even for Akira.

I had been walking in the general direction of the beach, through a rough field, when I tripped—in a hole, I noted, dazed.

I saw that my bare foot was bleeding, as well. I studied it closely, surprised to note that it wasn't one cut that had made it bleed, but many. And my other foot was bleeding, as well, lots of little tiny cuts and scrapes lining the bottom of both feet. I must have passed through some stickers without even feeling it. I still didn't feel it, in fact, so I just shrugged it off, and stood back up, continuing on to the beach. My left ankle was a little weak from the fall, so I had to favor my right strongly to keep walking. I didn't let up though, only stopping when I'd finally reached the beach. I had walked far, I noted. I couldn't even see Akira's house anymore from this beach.

I sank into the sand, curling into a sad little ball, like I had when I was upset as a child. Akira had always been there to comfort me, then. And he'd often been the only one who could, the only one I'd wanted to see, if I was upset or sad. But I'd learned to do without him for my entire adult life. It had been a sad life. I'd been so lonely, though I kept endlessly busy with work and family obligations.

I hadn't even tried to date in recent years, which seemed to be for the best. For me, at least. I didn't care to even try to become interested in men, much to my parents' dismay. They were desperate for grandchildren at this point in their lives, and my older brother and I seemed to be hopeless in that department. My brother was a shameless playboy. And I was a hopeless spinster, I was sure, from their exasperated point of view.

I fought it for a while, trying to keep myself a little numb, but eventually I just broke, sobbing softly into my hands. No matter how I looked at it, my future just looked so…empty, without Akira in it. I was so sick of feeling empty. And a few brief moments being full again only made me feel it more acutely.

I was a little stunned to see that it was fully dark as I lifted my wet hands from my tear-streaked face. I didn't have to look around again to know that I was utterly lost. I was too exhausted to care about my predicament, though. I curled back into my little ball, and fell into an exhausted sleep.

The sun was directly above me when I opened my sleepy eyes, immediately flinching back from the harsh light. It was several minutes before I mustered up the energy to rise to my feet. My whole body ached, my feet and ankle hurting with every step I took along the sandy beach. I couldn't believe that I had slept for so long. It had to be at least noon, going by the sun. I dug my phone out of my purse, not at all surprised to see that the battery had died.

I walked for maybe twenty minutes when I spotted some people on the beach. I hobbled to the family of three slowly but purposefully.

The mother, a heavy-set white woman, noticed me first, giving me a wide-eyed, surprised look. She elbowed her husband, pointing at me. I must have been a sight, by the concerned way they rushed to me, carrying their small child with them. I thought it was very nice, how concerned they were for an absolute stranger.

"Are you okay?" the woman asked, kind concern in every line of her face. I really didn't want to know how bad I must look at the moment, to elicit such a response. I just nodded, though I was far from all right. After being so sick the day before, and then laying in the hot sun for the duration of the morning, unprotected in the sand, I felt close to passing out.

I had to clear my dry throat several times before I could speak. "Do you have a phone that I could use? And could you tell me where I am?" I asked in a hoarse voice.

The worried couple was beyond helpful, rushing to give me their cell phone, and giving me very detailed directions to this spot of beach.

I called the hotel, directing the staff to send a driver to pick me up. Even the receptionist on the phone sounded worried. I supposed that I shouldn't have been surprised by that, since my luggage had arrived at the hotel a full day ago, and I had been conspicuously absent. I hoped that no one had contacted my father. He would worry needlessly. My mother would likely just shrug it all off, saying that I was a grown-up who could take care of myself.

The hotel car arrived very promptly, the couple hovering near me in concern all the while. I gave them my card. "Please, don't hesitate to call me, if you ever wish to stay at any of the Middleton hotels. You were a lifesaver for me today, and I would be happy to return the favor. I can arrange for comp rooms for you any time you need. Thank you," I told them, my voice stiff and formal. I didn't want to be so stiff with the nice couple, but it came out that way as all of my usual social graces were lost under the effort of simply trying not to pass out.

They eyed my card, seeming pleased with the offer. I sincerely hoped they took me up on it. I preferred, always, to repay my debts.

The driver from the day before, Thomas, picked me up. He was stunned speechless at the sight of me, opening the door for me without a word. "Ms. Middleton, can I take you to a hospital? You look unwell, if you don't mind my saying so."

I just shook my head stiffly. "Thank you, no. Please just drive me to the hotel. I'm quite fine." My tone was colder than I'd intended, but again, the effort to keep myself composed had robbed me of all social graces.

We weren't far from the hotel, arriving there in short minutes. Thomas held the car door open for me, his eyes concerned. "Can I help you, Ms. Middleton?" he asked.

I straightened as I stepped out of the car. "I just need my room key and number. That will be all, thank you."

It took an eternity for me to actually get to my room, my progress slow but determined. I leaned against the closed door, my eyes shutting in relief. *First, a bath*, I decided. I needed to eat, and to sleep, but I needed to be clean more than anything else just then.

I got in the large tub even as it filled with water. I didn't turn off the scorching flow until it was filled to the brim. I drifted off almost instantly.

The water was cold when I awoke, startled out of sleep by... something. I didn't know what, but I thought that it had been a noise. Only silence greeted me. I got stiffly out of the cold bath, resolving to get some actual work done.

I dressed in a cream-colored pencil skirt, paired with one of my countless white dress shirts. I tucked the shirt in, wanting to feel normal again, back in my business attire, and my business state of mind. I slipped on some electric blue Minolo stiletto's, veering as far as I could from the barefoot urchin I'd turned into after just a day back home. My feet were already killing me, so I figured why not give them a good reason to hurt? Cute shoes were a good reason.

I braided my hair back as tightly as my curls would go in the humid climate. I even made an attempt at makeup, though it was minimal.

A glance in the mirror told me that I looked infinitely better, my pink cheeks the only visible evidence of the rough day I'd had.

I made slow but sure progress to the hotel's large offices, going into the spacious, well-appointed office that was reserved for use only by the

Middleton family. I was aware of the startled glances I received as I walked, smoothly but slowly, past the office workers. I nodded politely to several faces that I recognized, but no one stopped my progress—thank God.

My desk was already covered in papers that needed either my approval or my signature, or both. I sat down heavily, getting to work. I was grateful for the distraction.

I worked for a good ten minutes without interruption. I thought it was unusual. Normally, when I visited one of the properties, I was practically mobbed with various local ideas and concerns. I didn't dwell on it long though, too grateful to just be left alone to work. Ten minutes was all I got, though.

A startled hand flew to my chest as a large figure burst through my door. An agitated Akira stood panting in front of me, his eyes running over me, his face wild and almost...scared.

CHAPTER
SIX

He lowered himself into the chair in front of my desk, his worried eyes never leaving me. "Are you all right?" he asked, his voice harsh. He was dressed in slacks and an uncharacteristically wrinkled white dress shirt. It brought attention to his beautiful brown skin.

I sighed, biting my lower lip so that it wouldn't quiver at the sight of him. I looked down as I answered, signing the paper I'd been studying. "I'm fine. Why do you ask?"

He cursed. I didn't look up. "Thomas called me. He said he'd picked you up from the beach, and that you looked as though you'd been attacked. What on earth happened? I've been looking for you ever since you disappeared from my house yesterday. I spent the night searching the beach for you. I had half of the island looking for you."

My gaze shot back to him at that, my eyes wide with shock. "I—I'm sorry. I didn't mean to worry anyone. As you can see, I'm perfectly fine."

His eyes widened, and I saw his temper rising by the way his muscles tensed up, his fists clenching. I watched that tension build in him with no small amount of fascination. His anger had never scared me, but it always got my attention.

"Tell me what happened," he said, his teeth clenched.

I flushed. "It's embarrassing, ok? But I'm fine now."

He just leaned forward, giving me his, 'I'm not backing down' look.

I sighed. "I went for a walk, barefoot, and scraped up my feet, then fell in a hole. It got dark, and I was lost, so I slept on the beach. In the morning, I found my way back. Nothing exciting, see?"

He buried his face in his hands as I spoke, rubbing his temples. "You slept all night on the beach, by yourself? Do you have any idea how unsafe that is?"

I wanted to pull out my hair; he was so frustrating. "I didn't *want* to sleep on the beach. Like I told you, I got lost."

"Why did you take off like that? I told you to wait outside." He didn't look up at me as he spoke, still rubbing his temples, but I could tell from his voice just how angry he was.

His words made *me* angry, as well. "Did you think that I was just going to wait patiently for you outside while you made up with your girlfriend?" I asked, trying to make my voice sound steady, instead of hurt.

His head snapped up at that, his eyes wild and baffled. "She's not my girlfriend."

I waved off his comment. "Whatever it is you call her, I didn't want to wait on standby while you went through your usual makeup/breakup routine with her." I stood up and took a step, intending to walk out of the room. I needed to escape to the restroom, or anywhere, really. I just needed to get out of his sight before I burst into tears.

The abuse I'd inflicted on my starved body in the last twenty-four hours presented itself at that moment, when I stood so fast that my vision went fuzzy. I swayed on my feet for an endless moment right before I collapsed into a dead faint.

I couldn't have been out for long. I was cradled in his arms when I came to, and we were still in the hotel, though Akira was striding out the door even as I roused.

"Where are we going?" I asked him in a weak voice.

He glanced down at me, his hard face showing relief that I was awake. "I'm taking you to the hospital."

I shifted in his arms, trying to get down. He just squeezed me tighter. "I don't need to go to the hospital. I probably just fainted from hunger," I told him, flushing. I felt like a particularly irresponsible child at the confession.

He blanched at my words, turning around to stride back into the hotel, heading straight into the promenade that led to the large selection of restaurants that the resort hosted. His face was hard and bleak, his mouth turned down in a stark frown, as he studied me. "When did you last eat?" he asked in a gruff voice.

"I ate at Tutu's yesterday, right before I ran into you. But I was... sick, right after I left your house, so I'm not sure if that counts."

His lower lip trembled a little, as though with strong emotion. I blinked up at him, wondering if I was seeing things. I was exhausted, dehydrated, and starving, so it wasn't much of a stretch to think that I might be having hallucinations.

"I'll order some food, and just eat it in my office. I need to get some things done, so I can set up the meetings that I came here for, before I head back to the mainland. You can put me down. I'm okay now."

He squeezed me tighter. "Just shut up, Lana."

My eyes snapped open in shock. Never in my life had he told me to shut up. It was so out of character for him that I actually obeyed.

He carried me into the first restaurant we came to. The staff recognized both of us on sight, and ushered Akira to a secluded table. He ordered as he walked. "She needs to eat immediately, so just bring us whatever is available right away."

"Yes, sir," the hostess said, striding away to comply.

He tried to set me in my own chair, but my arms just wrapped around his neck of their own volition.

He sighed, then sat. I sat up, turning until my back was against his chest, my head laid back against his shoulder. It felt so good, in spite of everything, just to be held in his massive arms. His arms had relaxed as I shifted on his lap, and I pulled them tightly around me again. He made a little humming noise, his cheek just touching the top of my head, and tightened those arms just how I wanted.

"You'll be the death of me, baby," he murmured against my hair. "Just what am I going to do with you?"

"I'll be gone soon enough. So nothing, I suppose," I said, feeling despondent at the thought.

His arms squeezed me. "Tell me about this mainland life you seem to need. Is it so much better for you, living in California?" His voice was very serious, as though he expected a very thorough answer.

Again, I thought it was unmercifully cruel for *him* to ask me that. I mulled over the question, feeling all of my old wounds as though they were fresh. "California? Is that where you think I live?" I asked, baffled by that. My parents lived there, and I traveled there frequently for work, but by no stretch of the imagination did I live there.

He gave me a little shake. "Your father and brother both told me that was where your residence was, when I asked them about you."

"You asked them about me?"

He tugged on a lock of my hair, hard. "Oww!" I told him.

"Of course I ask them about you. *You* don't talk to me. How else could I check up on you?" His tone was chiding, and I detected a genuine hurt in it as well. I was surprised into silence by the realization. *Had he expected me to call him?*

After all of the ways I had embarrassed the both of us, seducing him with absolutely no shame, and then professing my undying love for him afterward. He couldn't have been more clear about the fact that he could not return my feelings, and I had been mortified and devastated. He had felt guilty, and been embarrassed by the whole sordid thing. The thought had never even occurred to me that he would ever want anything to do with me again.

"So where do you live, then?" he asked after a long silence.

"I live…nowhere. I travel all the time. I work all the time. I stay on a lot of the resort properties, because it's just easier."

"So you have the flight gene, like your mother? You just like to stay on the move?" he asked, his tone probing. He wasn't trying to hurt me, I knew. He honestly thought that it was my choice to have no home.

"No," I said quietly. "I don't like it. It's bearable, sometimes, I suppose. But who gets to do what they want? That's what growing up is all about, right? Giving up the things that you really want."

He made that sympathetic sound in his throat that always made my throat thicken with unwanted tears. "Oh, Lana, I'm sorry to hear that. It was such a comfort to me through the years, thinking that, though we were missing you, at least you were living a life that made you happy."

I didn't answer. I couldn't. My mind was reeling. Was he trying to break my heart all over again? He had a knack for finding new and surprising ways to do it. Not only had I been miserable without his love, now I had to feel guilt that he was sad without my friendship.

"I would have called you if I knew that you wanted to talk to me," I told him. I realized, with a burst of bravado, that I wanted to stay in contact with him, wanted to be friends again, no matter how much it broke my heart.

"Oh, Lana." His voice was an anguished whisper against my hair. "You're breaking my heart, baby. How I must have hurt you, to have you thinking that I didn't want contact for all of these years. How could you ever think that?"

Our food arrived, the waitress nodding politely, but retreating quickly. We had to be an uncomfortable sight, me cuddled on his lap with tears in my eyes. It was two heaping plates of sausage and peppers rustica, with liberal portions of thick-crusted bread on the side.

"You never called me, either," I told him quietly.

He began to prepare a small bite for me, holding it up to my mouth, feeding me like a child. "I was the bastard who violated you, and then embarrassed you. And I know you overheard that unfortunate conversation I had with Milena. You had a good reason to hate *me*, so I did the only decent thing I could, and waited for you to contact me again when you were ready. I hated my birthdays every year after you left, because I always thought you'd call me. You used to make such a fuss over my birthdays, and some part of me just always hoped you'd soften towards me a little on that day. But I was so disappointed every time, even though I had no right to expect you to forgive me."

I was crying silently by the time he finished speaking, tears running liberally down my cheeks. I had hated his birthdays too, after I left. I had hated mine, as well. I always took a few days off for both of the dates, needing to be alone for the dark depression that always seemed to overtake me then.

Akira tore off a tiny piece of bread, holding it up to my mouth. I took the bite and chewed it, making myself eat, even though my appetite was nonexistent just then.

"I could never hate you, Akira. I could never even stay mad at you for more than a day, if you recall. Even when I tried very hard to."

He kissed my head, feeding me a tiny bite of sausage. "It warms my heart to hear that, Lana."

CHAPTER SEVEN

He fed me nearly half of the oversized plate before I cried uncle, and he let up on hand feeding me. He began to polish off the rest. I tried to move to the other chair so he could get better access to the food. The man had an unbelievable appetite. He always had. I wasn't about to get between him and his meal.

But his arm just tightened around my waist, holding me to him while he polished off everything left on the table with astonishing speed. He left no crust of bread uneaten.

I was giggling by the time he ate the last scrap of bread, dragging it around one of the plates, getting every last bit of pasta sauce. "I see you still eat a ridiculous amount of food."

He just grunted, tugging softly on a lock of my hair. "I'm three times the size of most people. Why shouldn't I eat accordingly?"

"Hmm, that's true. You wouldn't want that perfect bod to get scrawny."

"Are you making fun of me?" he asked, a smile in his voice.

I hadn't been, but his smile made me smile, and I suddenly did want to tease him. He had always been the best one to tease. Mari, Tutu, my brother Camden, and I had made a game out of it, and I'd always wanted to be the first one to make his mean face crack into a smile. And I usually had. "Of course not. Anything less than four thousand calories a day and you'd lose your position on the Swole Patrol. How embarrassing that would be for you."

He tickled me until I giggled helplessly. I saw heads turning to watch us out of the corner of my eye as we made a spectacle of ourselves. I couldn't summon up the will to care if we were making a scene. This felt like old times, happy times, and I was determined to savor it.

"Are you up for a trip to the beach?" he asked me suddenly, his tone serious. "We'll surf another day, when you're feeling better. I just want to watch the ocean with you."

I sighed, knowing I should stay at the hotel and work. And I should have been wary of the beach, considering the night I'd had, but I just couldn't turn down the chance to spend time with him. I'd never had that ability. And there was nothing in the world I'd rather do, than watch the ocean with Akira. "I'd love to."

We thanked the restaurant staff and left. I was walking on my own at that point, but Akira quickly took my arm hostage as we walked to his car.

Curiously, my hair came loose as we walked, and I glanced behind my shoulder, wondering how it had happened. I sent Akira a suspicious glare. He gave me a toothy white grin, holding up my hair tie without remorse. I elbowed him in the stomach. I thought it hurt my elbow more than it hurt his stomach, but he still threw me over his shoulder for the jab, smacking me soundly on the ass.

We were still in the hotel for that little spectacle, and I still couldn't bring myself to care, cursing him colorfully as I swatted at his back. He threw his head back and laughed at all of the things I came up with to call him. He brought my tirade to an abrupt end as I resorted to calling his mother nasty names. "I'm telling Tutu," he said quietly, a smile still strong in his voice. It shut me up, though. It wasn't smart to mess with Tutu. If you started a fight with Tutu, you lost. It was a well-known fact to the locals.

"I'll tell you what. If you promise to go surfing with me in the morning, I won't tell Tutu what you called her."

He dangled me farther down on his back as he spoke, tormenting me just because he could. It brought me into reach of his ass, so I didn't mind, smacking it as hard as I could. It hurt my palm, and he just spanked me right back. I spanked him again, softer this time, studying that perfect ass. I was convinced he had the best ass in the world. No one could convince me otherwise. It was perfectly shaped, and, well, perky. He had a perfectly rounded, perky butt. I squeezed it with both hands, and he pulled me higher, squeezing my own ass with one of his hands, in revenge.

"Deal. I'm not stupid enough to mess with Tutu. Now, put me down!"

He just laughed again. It was an evil sound.

"At least let me squeeze your butt some more, if you won't put me down," I teased.

He set me down then, but I saw that it was because we'd reached his car. He opened the door for me, and I bounced inside, feeling happier than I had in so long...

I cursed suddenly as I realized I'd forgotten my purse. It was still back in the office. I told Akira so.

He just shrugged. "I'll have one of my cousins bring it by when they get off work." Akira had about a million cousins, and many of them worked for our resort. I'd almost forgotten that, for some odd reason. I had been too long from the island.

Akira was quiet in the car, just shooting me occasional, concerned glances.

We had been driving for about ten minutes when I realized that we weren't headed to his house.

"What beach are we going to?" I asked him.

He sent me a small, happy smile. "Guess."

It didn't take me long to guess, since I remembered the island well, and I couldn't help but see exactly where he was going. "Oh, we can't, Akira. I don't even know if anyone's been taking care of the house. The yard is probably so overgrown that we won't even be able to navigate through it to get to the water."

His smile got bigger and wider, flashing me straight white teeth. "I've been taking care of it. It's as beautiful as ever."

I studied him, not sure what to think. "Has my father been making you? You know you don't have to do everything he asks."

He shook his head. "No, he never asked me to. I've just been doing it. I enjoy it, and I have cleaners come in every week to do the cleaning."

"You've been doing that this whole time?"

He nodded, taking a deep breath. "Ever since you left."

"Why?"

"I told you, I enjoy it. But also, I guess it was always just wishful thinking. I never wanted to lose hope that you would come back, and when you did, I wanted your little slice of paradise to stay just how you remembered it."

I had to look away, touched to the point of tears by his actions.

He gripped my hand in his. It was so warm, and I clutched it tight.

We arrived at the long, private drive that led to my family's island estate. I'd known that I missed the place, but as we approached the house, it was driven home to me just how much. As a kid, I'd thought I'd be living here forever. If anyone would have suggested otherwise, I'd have been baffled, and possibly burst into tears. This was home. This island and this house.

The house was a colossal, modern villa, with pale stone built into clean lines, and huge windows showcasing the glory of the nature surrounding it.

We went through the house to get to the backyard. We didn't linger in the house long, but everything looked to be how I'd left it. It even smelled of plumerias, as I remembered.

"Oh, hey, hold up," Akira said as I pushed the button that opened a huge panel at the back of the house up to the elements.

I glanced back at him. He held up a tiny island dress, bikini, and flip-flops that he had clutched in one hand. I'd seen him ruffling through the back of his SUV when we'd arrived, but I hadn't seen what he was grabbing.

I smiled at him. "Thanks." I grabbed them from him, heading past him to the nearest room to change in.

He grabbed my arm, grinning. "It's just the two of us, Lana. Do you really need privacy?"

I raised my brows at his about-face. Taking his question as a challenge, I stepped out of my shoes, unzipping my skirt to let it drop around my ankles. I unbuttoned my shirt, and had my bra unclasped before he could do more than stare. I'd never been shy with my body. Growing up on the island, spending every day in a bikini, it had never even occurred me to cover up. And frankly, I knew his reaction to my stripping would be gratifying. I was not disappointed. His jaw dropped as I got out of my clothes in record time.

I got dressed nearly as quickly, slipping on the bikini, shrugging into the dress, and slipping into the flip-flops while he just watched me, looking hot and flustered, which was how I liked him best of all.

I gave him a radiant smile. "Ready." I grabbed his hand, tugging him with me outside. He didn't resist.

I didn't even pause at the pool, going directly for the long trail that led into the lush green forest and to our private beach.

Akira stopped me at the forest line, reaching to pluck a white plumeria from one of many trees that dotted our property. He smiled as he tucked into my left ear, then started walking again.

"Wrong side," I told him, feeling silly. Of course he knew that a plumeria over the left ear meant I was taken, and one on the right meant I was looking. Mari had been the one to teach me, years ago.

"I don't think so."

I felt my heart turn over in my chest with a fearful kind of hope. "Oh?" I asked in a weak voice. "Why don't you think so?"

He sent me a suspiciously innocent look. "Well, you're not looking for a man, are you? A flower on the right side means you want every interested guy to hit on you."

I supposed he had a point, since that was the last thing I wanted. I fingered the flower as we made our way from the small patch of lush forest that led to the ocean. "It's as beautiful as I remember," I told him, taking in the enchanted green serenity around me.

"Yes," he said simply.

The black sand beach was just as I'd remembered it, too. And the ocean. Oh, the ocean. I'd always had such a fascination with that endless expanse of blue, and I always found it to be the most beautiful right at sunset, which was fast approaching.

Akira sat in the sand, pulling me between his spread legs without a word. I leaned back against his chest, thinking that this was my own perfect little slice of paradise.

"I think I could stay like this forever, with you," I told him quietly.

He pressed a cheek against my hair, wrapping his arms around my shoulders. "Why don't you, then? Give me one good reason why you can't stay on this rock?"

My breath grew ragged, and I couldn't seem to find the breath to speak. I'd been so brave when I was younger, declaring my feelings with no hesitation or reservation whatsoever. It seemed as though I'd just used it all up back then, with none of it left for the grown-up me. It made me sad, but I still couldn't seem to ask him the questions I wanted to. Could I just stay here? Was it a terrible idea, or a brilliant one? I couldn't live my life based on whether or not Akira could love me like I did him. I knew that was not way to live. But could I live here, and see him every day, and be able to endure the longing, if we weren't together?

"I'll have to think about it," I told him quietly, watching the sky turn brilliant with the sunset.

He nuzzled his face into my neck, placing a soft kiss there. "You do that."

"You want me to stay?" I asked him, holding my breath to hear his answer.

"Yes," he said thickly. "I want that." He cleared his throat.

We were both silent for a long time, watching the sky turn colors in a glorious display that had never failed to move me.

"This place has the most beautiful sunset in the world," I murmured.

"Yes. The beach for sunset, and Haleakala for sunrise. Guess where we're going in the morning?"

I turned my head to give him an amused smile. "You really want to wake up at four a.m. to catch the sunrise?"

"More like three, and yes, we're going. It's been years since either of us has seen a Haleakala sunrise, and I think it's fitting that we go together."

I snuggled my back into his chest, feeling a wave of contentment wash over me. Even if the world ended tomorrow, I thought I could be okay with it, after having watched this perfect sunset, and after, a perfect sunrise with the love of my life.

It only took one small stroke of his thumb against my collarbone to change the mood from sweet to hot in an instant.

He kissed just the perfect spot on my neck, his hands finding and kneading at my breasts with just the right pressure. I moaned.

"You're going to ride me reverse cowgirl," he murmured into my ear. "So you can watch the sunset while I make you come. You will never forget this ride."

"Sex on the beach? Isn't that messy?" I asked ruefully, but I was so game. "We'll get sand in our unmentionables."

"Maybe. It won't be so bad if you're on top, but it will probably be messy, and God only knows where we'll be finding sand later. Do you mind?" As he spoke, he was shifting me against him, lifting me higher so that he could slide his hips under me, parting my legs to straddle him.

I was already untying my bikini bottoms as he opened his slacks, freeing himself. "I do not. I can't believe you wore a dress shirt and slacks to the beach, Akira."

He didn't respond, but I heard a harsh gasp behind me as I lined myself up over his stiff length. I was already wet, desire only taking the briefest thought for me when it came to Akira.

I circled my hips, wetting his tip.

He groaned loudly.

I worked him into me slowly. I had no choice with his size and the angle. He was so thick that I held my breath as I worked the last few inches inside of me. I sucked in a rough breath when I was finally seated to the hilt, stuffed full of him.

I just stayed like that for a while, adjusting to the size and the angle, which felt even more wonderful with every breath I took, and watched the sunset.

"You're missing the sunset in this position," I gasped at him.

His hands stroked my hips, kneading at my flesh. "I'm not missing anything, baby," he rasped. "Most beautiful view I've ever had in my life."

I shuddered at his words, and began to move, pushing on my knees to lift up and forward, then down and back to reseat myself. We both cried out loudly.

"You feel so good, Akira. You're so big, but it feels so good."

"You're so fucking tight, Baby. I don't know how long I'll last, but I want to stay inside of you for days."

I whimpered, lifting up again, the delicious slide of him dragging along every sensitive nerve inside of me. "I won't last days, Akira. I don't even think I'll last minutes like this."

He grunted. "Good. Me too. I intend to spend as much time inside of you as possible, and I have no problem trying until we get it right."

I ground back down onto him, then dragged up again, my movements getting faster.

He gripped my hips tighter, moving his hips to take over the movements. I was fine with that, since he built us into just the right rhythm, pounding into me.

My head fell back, but I kept my eyes open on the brilliant sky as I came, shivers of ecstasy rocking my body as the sky continued to give me the show of a lifetime. I cried out his name hoarsely, unable to even try to keep it in.

He shouted my name, bottoming out inside of me with one last hard slam, his hard hands on my hips all that kept me upright.

It took long minutes for us both to recover. We covered the essentials and settled back into watching the sky and the ocean again.

I sighed contentedly as the last brilliant streaks of gold faded from the sky.

It was a perfect night, very little of it spent sleeping. I thought that Akira had elicited every last orgasm inside of me by the time I drifted into a deep, but short, sleep.

He was waking me again way too soon.

"No. Humans need to rest, Akira."

"I know, Lana. You just need to bundle up and get into the car. I'll do all the driving, and you can sleep until we reach the top of Haleakala.

"Fine," I said grumpily, sitting up. We'd ended up sleeping in my old bedroom, and I raided the closet for jeans and a sweatshirt.

We were in the car and driving within fifteen minutes, and I leaned my chair back, promptly falling back to sleep.

I grumbled when he woke me again, calling him a few nasty names as I woke up what seemed like an instant later.

Of course, I had to take it all back as I watched the sun rising in what I was convinced was the most beautiful sunrise in the world. Streaks of gold painted the clouds that hovered just below us. Cradled in Akira's arms, I knew that this was the closest to paradise I'd ever been.

CHAPTER EIGHT

"Let's go hang out at the bar," he murmured into my ear later that afternoon. We'd spent the morning surfing. The saltwater had stung the crap out of my feet at first, but I hadn't made a peep. I wouldn't miss out on a day of surfing with Akira for any amount of discomfort.

I stiffened, because Milena worked there. He seemed to read my thoughts. "Milena is taking some time off. She's been too unstable lately to even work."

I agreed easily enough. I'd never pass up on a chance to see Tutu and Mari.

We reached the stretch of Kalua shops quickly, sharing a companionable silence in the car. Akira opened the door for me before I'd even unbuckled my seat belt. He had always been like that, always the gentleman for me; even when I was ten, when he'd called me a 'little lady', as he opened it with a flourish. I had secretly loved the title.

The bar was already crowded, even though it was early afternoon. I realized that it was Friday. This place had always been hopping on Friday night. Two spaces at the full bar magically opened up when a few locals saw that Akira wanted us to sit there. He nodded at them respectfully. They nodded back, not having to explain. It was a fact that Akira Kalua got and gave respect in these parts. No words needed to be exchanged.

He ordered a beer, looking at me when the bartender asked what for the lady. I smiled at the friendly man, not recognizing him at all. It didn't mean that he was new, I supposed. It just meant that he wasn't more than eight years into the job. There was a time when I would have known everyone here. Even as an underage teenager, I'd practically lived here. He was a local. He had a slight build and friendly brown eyes. He was the opposite of Akira looks-wise, looking harmless with his nice smile. "Just water, thank you."

Akira gave me a disgusted look, his mean upper lip curling at me. "That's borin'."

I laughed. "What? Are you disappointed that I won't be getting drunk and letting you take advantage of me?"

It was a score. He almost blushed at the comment. I leaned forward to whisper in his ear. "You know I don't have to be drunk for that. You can search me on the internet anytime you like, and have your way with your filthy palm."

He grabbed me, tickling me unmercifully for the taunt. There were tears running down my face before he let me loose, a grin on his face.

I knew without having to look around that we had the attention of the bar crowd. I didn't care. I smiled back at him, a happy twinkle in my eye that had been absent for at least eight years. "I know, when you torture me that much, that I hit a nerve."

He was smiling at me unreservedly, a smile that was rare and that I treasured. His eyes were soft, and he just looked…happy. "Come here," he said, pulling me against him and kissing the top of my head.

We separated quickly from the embrace, both suddenly self-conscious. I resumed my own seat, taking a drink of my water.

He clucked his tongue at me. "At least get a soda or somethin'. That is just a sad thing to drink at a bar."

I just shrugged. "I don't like soda. I guess I wouldn't mind tea."

He rose, kissing the top of my head again, as though he couldn't help it. "I'll be right back. Tutu has the best tea next door. You still take it plain?"

I nodded, my eyes following his every move as he strode across the room. A few familiar locals stopped to greet me, as though they'd been intimidated to approach when Akira was there.

I smiled and chatted with them, catching up a bit.

When Akira returned, he brought my tea, and Tutu. They were a sight, mother and son, one so massive, the other the definition of petite. It always made me smile, because the tiny one called the shots. Akira was a respectful, dutiful son.

She was all smiles, in a doozy of a mood, at her most benevolent. It made all of us a little wary. You had to worry a bit, when Tutu was that happy. She hugged me, a seat magically vacating itself so she could sit beside me. She gave Akira a pointed look. "Well? What are you waiting for? Go work the café. I need to talk to my granddaughter."

He gave her a borderline unfriendly look, but sure enough, he obeyed.

Tutu turned her regard to me, and I was almost scared at her intense expression.

Tutu hadn't liked me at first, when I began to dog Akira's heels as a child. She'd called me a haole, and ignored me. I hadn't gone away, so eventually, she had started to talk to me. At first, I'd just gotten lectures about how Maui should belong to the locals again, and how men like my father were the problem. She had scared me as a child, so I hadn't argued with her, not even to defend my dad. I had just nodded solemnly, as though I understood what she was saying well enough to agree. I hadn't, but she had taken my agreement as respect. And so our special bond began. I grew on her over the years with my earnest perseverance. She respected my persistence, and my audacity, and I respected *her*. I had desperately wanted her approval.

I was around ten when I began to tell anyone who would listen that I was going to marry Akira when I grew up. Tutu hadn't liked that. She had been mad at me whenever I worked up the nerve to repeat it to her. But I'd respected her, so I had wanted her to know my intent. She had finally berated me so soundly for it that I had run to Akira, crying. I had explained it to him, and he had been sympathetic, taking me back to the formidable woman so that we could make up.

Tutu had patted my head affectionately then. "It's not your fault, Lana. You're not a local; you can't help that. Akira needs to marry a local girl. It's our way."

I had been crying, but I had stood my ground, anyway. "But I want to be in your family!" I had told her in an angry little voice.

She had studied me with a little smile. She was a diabolical woman, so even that smile had been a little scary to a ten-year-old. "I'll tell you what. I don't have any grandkids, because of my worthless children." She had paused there to send Akira a long, malevolent glare. He'd smirked, unaffected. "But you are a lovely child. I've never seen a little girl more beautiful than you. Your purple eyes make me think you might have magic, which is very good. *And* you're smart. *And* you're a stubborn little thing. *And* I like your backbone. *And* I think you're just ornery enough to be a Kalua. So, you may have the distinct honor of calling me Tutu. It means grandma."

I'd looked at Akira, wanting him to approve. He'd smiled warmly at me, and I was ecstatic. I knew it was the biggest accomplishment of my young life, being the first to call her Tutu.

"So you're family now. Perhaps Akira will be less worthless and stupid when you're finally a grown-up." I looked at Akira as she spoke.

His nose had just wrinkled at her, his only answer. The look said - 'Not happening'.

Tutu had continued, thankfully ignoring the look. "And *since* you're family now, and therefore a local, I will approve of the marriage."

I had been on cloud nine for ages after being added to my favorite family. Akira and Mari had turned it into a bit of a joke, and took to calling her Tutu, as well. They said that since she wanted grandkids so badly, that everyone should just call her Tutu, since neither of them planned to ever get married. Soon, all of the locals took up the habit of calling her Tutu, and she had taken to the title as though that was what she had wanted all along.

CHAPTER NINE

Tutu brought me back to the present by leaning forward to press her nose and forehead against mine. It was an affectionate gesture, one you would give a granddaughter. I smiled at her fondly as she pulled back to study me. "You know, I'm old and stubborn, and I decided a long time ago that I'm too old to have to change my mind about anything. I get to be set in my ways now. It's the law. But I have decided to change my mind about one thing. I wasn't wrong about it. I've just changed my mind. Your haole dad is not the problem with Maui."

I raised my brows at her, wondering where this was going. I had always suspected that she was secretly grateful to my dad for being a mentor to Akira, but she would never admit it. Or so I had thought.

"He isn't the problem, because he had you. And if you have Akira's babies, lots of them preferably, then they will inherit back some of our land for us. So you see, your dad is only some of the problem with Maui."

I smiled at her weakly, uncomfortable talking with her about anything to do with Akira, now that I was grown. It was obvious that my promise to marry him would not be kept, at this point.

She just patted me on the shoulder and stood. "I just needed to get that off my chest. I might die tomorrow, so you should listen to me. I might haunt you forever if you don't."

That one made me laugh, my discomfort passing. I had heard that famous Tutu quote many a time. It was one of my favorites. Even as a child, when the thought of being haunted had been kind of scary, I had still felt a little comforted by the notion of Tutu staying near me forever.

Akira was grimacing as he re-joined me. He studied me. "Tutu was giving me the most evil cackle when she sent me back in. You okay? What crazy thing did she say to you?"

I just shook my head, smiling. "Just some Tutu wisdom. She's in rare form today. She even threw her, 'I might die tomorrow, I'll haunt you forever,' line at me. Cantankerous as ever."

That made him laugh. I touched the dimple in his cheek as he did so. I couldn't seem to help it, my hand had a mind of its own. And his eyes got so soft when I did that. He shocked me by pulling me snugly into his arms, placing a sweet kiss on top of my head. When he didn't immediately release me, I just went with his affectionate mood, throwing both of my arms around his neck, and burrowing my face into my favorite spot on his chest. I knew the bar crowd was staring at us. Akira was not exactly known for being a demonstrative, affectionate man. Just the opposite, in fact. But he had always been different for me. Everyone had probably just forgotten that. I *had* been gone a long time.

He was in a kind mood, and so let me stay like that for a long time, my cheek on his chest, his hand stroking over my hair. I felt him playing with the streaky waves. He even brought a lock to his lips at one point.

I wanted to stay like that forever, crowded bar or not. I felt cherished like that.

We didn't speak for a long time. I didn't even consider it. I didn't want to risk breaking the spell. He took long drinks of his beer, but never relinquished his hold on me, and didn't push me away. I wasn't planning to move an inch if he didn't make me.

"Do you want me to get you more tea?" Akira murmured, his mouth close to my ear as he spoke.

I made a non-committal noise into his shirt. "Maybe later."

His hands stroked my back. "I need to go tell Mari that you're here, anyway. She'll never forgive me if you come here to hang out and she doesn't even know about it. I'll be right back, k?" He set me away from him as he spoke, and I sat back down in my chair, already missing that warm embrace. He kissed my head before he left.

Milena must have had someone on the watch-out for him to leave, because just seconds after he'd left the bar, she was taking his seat beside me. She glared at me malevolently. I recognized that she was beautiful. But I had never understood why Akira was with her, other than that. He could have had anyone. And she was rude and mean, and overly aggressive. I had never understood their relationship, but I'd always hated it.

"You think you're special to him, but you're not. You're nothing but his little puppy," she said in a vicious voice.

I just sighed at her weak attack. Really, she could have done better. It wasn't hard to hurt my feelings where Akira was concerned, but she had somehow managed to miss a very large target.

"Did you have a point? He says you're not his girlfriend anymore," I said, wanting to hear her take on that.

She flushed. "Not now, I'm not. But he was mine for years, haole.

How long did you get him for? A night or two? Just think of how good those nights were, and then think of a thousand nights like that. That's what I got from him. You got nothing. You are nothing. And yet you have the nerve to disrespect me."

I raised my brows at her. "How so? I think I do a pretty good job of staying out of your way, which is what you clearly prefer."

I saw her getting visibly more agitated at my words. That hadn't been my intention. I wasn't trying to make her mad. I just wanted her to go away.

She pointed a red tipped finger at me. "You fucked him when he was my man, back when you were eighteen. I heard you talking about it, so you can't even deny it."

I froze at that accusation, because it actually hurt. "You were broken up at the time," I told her, lifting my chin.

That sharp nail poked me in the chest, hard. It stung. Her voice was a near-shout when she responded, "That breakup was his idea, and I didn't agree to it! And, since we got back together a few months later, that breakup didn't even count. So you fucked my man!" As she spoke, her nail jabbed hard into my chest several times to emphasize her point.

My eyes widened. So they had been broken up when he'd made love to me the first time. I hadn't been sure of that, after overhearing a conversation they'd had the day after he'd been with me. The idea that he'd lied to me about something like that had haunted me for years. I was so relieved to find that he really hadn't lied.

I just looked at her steadily, determined to pretend her sharp pokes didn't sting like a bitch. "Do you have any idea how crazy you sound right now? If someone breaks up with you, that is called being *broken up*. You don't have to agree to it for it to count."

Her eyes widened and I saw the moment her crazy switch snapped on, her eyes going wild, her fingernails flying at my face.

I'd never been in a fight before, but I'd seen quite a few of them, and I'd always looked down on the girls that used their nails, or went for the hair. I had always told myself that if I ever had to fight somebody, I'd use my fists, goddammit.

It was pure instinct that had me slapping my hand to her forehead before those mean nails could reach my face. I was taller, so my reach was better. It was that simple. But it hurt like crazy when she started scratching at my arm like a wild animal. I fisted my free hand, almost excited to try my first real punch on somebody. Especially since that someone was Milena. I swung at her face, since her cheek was practically asking me to. It was pointing right at me.

It didn't knock her out cold, unfortunately, as I'd been sort of fantasizing it would. It didn't really even slow her down. I made solid enough contact that it hurt my hand, but it only seemed to piss her off more, if that was possible.

She finally got ahold of my hair, in spite of my better reach. She yanked a hunk out, hard, calling me every nasty name in the book. I had a few choice words for her as well, the most prevalent one starting with a C.

I punched her again, in the head that time. *Oww*. That one definitely hurt my hand more than it hurt her head. I quickly resorted to hair pulling, my punching skills sorely lacking.

I gripped the top of her hair, trying to ignore what she was doing to my arm, even though it hurt like hell. I had a sudden spark of inspiration. My fists were a no go, but my knee might be hard enough to do some damage. I bent my injured elbow, pulling her a little closer, and raising my knee up into her stomach with the same motion.

Score! I thought. It knocked the breath out of her, and I did it again, just because my arm was wet with blood from her evil claws, and it still hurt like a motherfucker.

I was getting ready to knee her again when she was torn away from me. I met Akira's frantic eyes as he grasped her around the middle, pulling her away from me. His eyes ran over me, widening when he saw the bloody scratches that covered my arm. He cursed as he pulled her farther from me.

Big arms wrapped around me from behind. I realized that it was some man who thought I was going to try to attack Milena even after she'd been pulled off me. I hadn't even considered the idea. I saw Akira's eyes as the man put hands on me. It was a scary sight. They went from frantic, straight to bat-shit crazy, his own crazy switch snapping on. Akira was about to blow. He spared one of the arms holding a furiously struggling Milena to point it at the man directly behind me. "Get your fucking hands off her!" he barked at him. The man released me instantly.

Akira eyed the crowded bar, his look a warning. "If anyone else lays so much as a fucking finger on her, I'm going to jail tonight!" Akira shouted to the room at-large before pulling his psycho ex out the door.

Akira came back inside less than five minutes later, looking positively volatile. His eyes were still wild as he approached me.

I was sitting in my same chair by the bar, Mari and Tutu hovering over me, carefully rolling up the sleeve of my scratched-up arm to see how bad it was. Other than a missing hunk of hair, it was the only part of my body she had managed to reach. I was kind of proud of the fact. So were Mari and Tutu, going by their excited chatter.

"Milena's been in lots of fights, but I'd say you won, pretty girl," Mari was saying, more concerned with establishing my victory than with the actual fight. I couldn't help but smile at her enthusiasm.

Tutu nodded sagely. "I always knew it," she said, as though she had predicted the whole thing and knew exactly how it would turn out. It was typical Tutu.

Mari and I shared an amused look.

Akira's first good look at the deep gouges in my arm had him turning away. He strode to the nearest wall, pulled back his arm, and punched a hole in it. It was a very impressive display of both his rage and his strength. I wanted to tease him about it, but knew that it was too soon to try joking with him like that.

His eyes were less wild but just as agonized when he approached me again. "I'm so sorry, baby." He squeezed in to embrace me, completely ignoring his mother and sister, who were both cursing him for taking their spots.

He kissed the top of my head. "Come on, Lana. You need to have those cleaned up at the hospital."

I let him pull me gently to my feet by my good hand. Mari and Tutu shouted advice at him as he pulled me to the door.

"Get back to work," he shouted back, ushering me outside.

He was very quiet in the car, using one hand to drive, the other one warmly gripping my knee. The touch was meant to be comforting, but it was still an instant turn-on for me. I used the hand of my uninjured arm to inch the loose skirt of my sundress up my legs, parting them as I did so. Akira shot me a stern look, but didn't fight me when I slid his hand higher, onto my inner thigh. I worked the material of my dress high, until I was exposed enough to shove his hand just where I wanted it.

He stroked me with a soft touch, though his eyes were still hard as he gave me a censorious look. "You are incorrigible," he told me, plunging a thick finger inside of me. He stopped the divine motion almost immediately, since we were already pulling into the hospital parking lot.

"I won the fight," I told him proudly as he pulled me out of the car by my good hand. I wanted him to know that, in case he hadn't noticed when he was breaking it up.

He glared at me. "You shouldn't have *been* fighting in the first place," he told me with his best lecturing tone.

I glared back. "You think I started that? I was just defending myself. Your ex is a psycho, but I still won."

His face tightened harshly enough that I felt it pull at the strings on my heart. I could see, just from his face, that he was blaming himself for the whole sordid fiasco. "It's my fault. I shouldn't have left your side. I was so sure she wouldn't show. I warned her that if she came to the bar while you were in town, or laid so much as a finger on you, that she'd lose her job. I thought surely that would be enough to keep her from trying to harm you, but she either didn't believe me, or just didn't care."

I was shocked. "So you fired her?"

He nodded, his face hard. "And you need to press charges. She needs to know that she can't touch you."

I mulled it over. Our fight had been unwelcome, and my arm hurt like hell, but Milena losing her job over it seemed like enough of a punishment, to me. "I'm not going to. If you fired her, I think that's enough of a punishment."

He looked like he wanted to argue with me, but he stayed silent, pulling me to the hospital entrance. "I still hate her guts, though," I continued. "I'm so jealous of her that I can barely stand it."

He looked genuinely surprised by my confession. I couldn't imagine why he'd be surprised by it. "Why on earth would you be jealous of her?" he asked.

"She told me she'd had a thousand nights with you, and I only got two. One and a half, rather. I hate her guts for that. And knowing you two, you'll probably reconcile again in a week."

He gave me a very annoyed look as he opened the door for me. "That's ridiculous, Lana. We've been broken up for years. Though I guess you wouldn't know it by how she still acts. I can't understand why she can't get over it. We were never good for each other, and over the years, we only got worse. She resented me for what I couldn't feel for her, and if I'm brutally honest, I only stayed with her for so long because I thought that I didn't deserve better. I ended it years ago, though, when I realized that I'd much rather be alone than with someone who brought out the worst in me. Milena is a bitter woman who can't grow up enough to let go of the past. The very distant past, at that. You have nothing to be jealous of."

I mulled that one over. She wasn't the only woman who couldn't let go of the very distant past. His assessment wounded me, because even though he'd been referring to Milena, I knew that I was no different. I wanted to let go, but I didn't seem to have that ability. I wished to God that I did. Unwillingly, my mind wandered back to the past.

CHAPTER TEN

8 YEARS AGO

When Akira had asked me what I wanted him to get me for my eighteenth birthday, I hadn't even had to think about it. I wanted *him*. Though I was smarter than to tell him that. Instead, I had asked him to spend the day with me. He agreed without hesitation, though he stubbornly insisted that I couldn't call it a date.

He hadn't had to ask me how I wanted to spend the morning. That one was a no-brainer. We spent it in the ocean, catching waves for endless hours. I had straddled my board a lot, practicing provocative poses, trying to tempt him, as I had taken to doing a lot recently. But today, it was different. I was a grown-up today, and there was no reason for Akira not to touch me now.

I arched my back when he looked at me, thrusting my full breasts forward in my tiny lavender bikini. It was literally the tiniest one I could find, barely covering the essentials. He gave me his stern, 'knock it off' look, and went back to studying the waves.

When he'd seen me walk out wearing the minuscule suit, he'd just raised his brows and said, "I guess you want to watch me get into some fights on your birthday." His tone had been dark, his face forbidding, but I had beamed at him, taking it as a good sign.

He watched the waves for a good ten minutes after he'd given me 'the look', then finally, I'd resorted to drastic measures. I had gone to great lengths to assure that I didn't have a tan line for tonight, wanting my body to look perfect for him. I'd been tanning naked in my back yard, so the feeling of the soft breeze on my bare chest was not all that foreign to me as I untied the top of my suit, letting it fall down to my waist. I studied the waves, as Akira did, pretending not to notice the slip.

I felt my breasts tighten the second that he saw what had happened. He started cursing. "Lana, your top!" he snapped at me.

I looked down at my chest, acting baffled, as though I couldn't imagine what could have happened to it. He was still cursing as he straddled his own board, paddling over to me to fix it himself, since I was being too slow about it. I glanced around as he covered my breasts with the tiny triangles of material. I tried to look worried. "Do you think anyone saw?"

He glanced around, his face thunderous, ready to stare down, or possibly pound, any poor fool he caught looking. But there was no one. We were virtually alone, all of the other surfers far enough away that they couldn't have gotten a good look.

"Will you tie it for me, Akira? I guess I didn't tie it tightly enough."

He tied it at my neck without a word. The triangles didn't fall into place on their own though, so I was still exposed. I made no move to cover up, so he did that too, moving the thin material over my hard nipples, cursing all the while.

I didn't bother with the trick again. It obviously hadn't worked, so the rest of the morning was spent surfing and basking. I spent most of it watching Akira. He was so magnificent that I could have watched him forever.

We didn't get back to his house until mid-afternoon. I used his tiny downstairs shower to wash off all of the sand and salt and sea, and Akira used his master bath upstairs to do the same. I had toyed with the idea of slipping into his shower with him and seducing him there, but decided against it. It didn't seem fair to sneak in on him like that.

He was lounging on his back on his lived-in sofa when I re-emerged from the bathroom. He was wearing some soft athletic shorts, black with a white stripe down the side, and nothing else, his glorious chest bare. He didn't glance up at me as I came to see what he was watching on TV. That was fortunate, since I might have lost my nerve if he had looked at what I was wearing, right at first.

I was wearing a micro-mini pleated red plaid skirt, and a small, short sleeved, white button down shirt with it. It was a naughty schoolgirl look that I had seen Milena wear a few times, and so figured Akira must like the look. Mine had a few extra naughty modifications, like no panties or bra, and all of the buttons undone on my top. It gaped open, exposing my full, tan breasts with their tiny, coral-colored nipples.

"What do you wanna do now, birthday girl?" Akira asked without looking up.

I bit my lip, deciding to go for it with gusto. I was straddling his prone figure before he could blink, lining my panty-less sex along his soft shorts.

His eyes flew open wide in shock, staring at my exposed breasts as though he didn't have a clue what they were. I was unbelievably gratified when I felt him growing hard against me. Instinctively, I started to rub myself against him, finding the material of his shorts to be soft against my bare skin.

I was a virgin. In fact, I'd never even kissed a guy, since Akira wouldn't kiss me. But I had a filthy mind and a filthy mouth, and I'd learned all I'd thought there was to know on the internet. It was one of my favorite pastimes lately, finding some new and shocking thing on the internet, then using it to shock Akira. His face turned purple sometimes, when I disturbed him enough with my latest findings. I would get a thirty-minute lecture after that, but it was always worth it. I'd always liked even his sternest lectures.

I moaned as he just kept growing against me. I could tell he was big, even without looking. He felt massive and hard as a rock as I moved my sex against him, arching my back to rub him on a spot that felt particularly divine. He just watched me, looking like a deer in headlights. I reached into the elastic waistband of his shorts, gripping him with my hand, and he gasped. I made a little sound of pleasure in my throat. I loved the feel of him so much. He was so hard, but the skin on his cock was so smooth, like velvet. I shoved his shorts down, using my hand to rub his now bare erection along my slick passage.

That got a reaction, and he sat up, pushing me off his lap. I sprawled out on the floor, a little stunned. It had knocked the wind out of me. Akira cursed, then apologized, but made no move to help me up. He looked like he was almost afraid of me. He sat watching me, his elbows on his knees now, shorts again covering his magnificent erection.

I propped myself up on my elbows, my breasts jutting forward. I drew up my knees, parting them a little so that he could see my sex clearly. "I know what I want for my birthday now," I told him. I began to touch my sex as I spoke, looking down at the wet folds as I did so.

"No," he said, obviously reading my intent. "We can't do that, Lana. It's completely inappropriate."

I pouted at him. "You didn't even let me finish. Don't you want to hear what I was going to say?"

He shook his head, his jaw clenched. *Stubborn man.*

I looked down again at myself as I pushed a finger inside. "Do you think my pussy is pretty, Akira?" I asked, wanting to shock him and turn him on with the crude language. "I know men are supposed to love them, but I don't think mine's very cute. Do you think it is?"

His face looked in danger of turning purple, but he couldn't seem to look away from what I was doing with my hand.

I stood, shrugging out of my shirt. It hadn't been covering anything anyway. "I was going to say, before you rudely interrupted me, that I wanted you to kiss me. Just a kiss. I want you to be my first."

I approached him as I spoke, and he sat up straight to watch me. I walked until I bumped into his chest, my legs straddling one of his. My breasts were dangerously close to his face. I brushed them against him, once, twice. "Will you be my first kiss, Akira?" I whispered.

He didn't answer. I straddled his legs, my knees digging into his soft couch. I tightened them on his hips as I leaned forward to kiss him.

I grabbed his hair as I did so, and he didn't stop me, still frozen in place. I rubbed against him like a kitten, groaning, and he finally reacted, gripping my hair and kissing me back. He tasted divine, and his mean lips were so soft against mine. I felt such an aching emptiness at my core, and I wanted so badly for him to be inside of me, to fill that emptiness. I rubbed my sex against his hard length until we both moaned.

The kiss went on and on, and I was more than ready for the next step when I finally pulled back. "Thank you," I told him, panting. "That was exactly how I dreamed my first kiss would be. Now I want you to make love to me." As I spoke, I brought his hands up to my aching breasts, and he kneaded at the pliant flesh, his eyes intense. I loved watching his dark hands against my skin, the contrast so beautiful to me.

Abruptly, his hands left me, and he pushed me back up to my feet with hard hands on my hips. "We can't do this, Lana. This is *wrong*," he told me, his voice harsh and labored.

I propped my foot up beside his hip, giving him a hell of a view in my micro-mini skirt. I gripped one of his hands, slipping it between my legs to touch me. He didn't resist me, immediately beginning to touch me just how I craved, his fingers skillful in their soft exploration. "I'm eighteen today, Akira. There's no reason why you can't take me now."

He had a hard finger pushed inside of me, just the tip, as he spoke in a breathless voice. "There are a million reasons, the first of which is that you deserve better than me, Lana. You're made of too fine of stuff for the likes of me. And I respect your father. He's trusted me to spend countless hours with you, over the years. I'm positive that he wouldn't approve of me doing *this* with you."

As he spoke, I wiggled against his big finger, ignoring all of those reasons out of hand. They were ridiculous, to me. I was an adult today, and I would do what I wanted. I pushed down on his finger, and he worked it deeper, groaning as he did so. "You're too tight, Lana. I would hurt you."

He pulled his shorts down, exposing his engorged member. "Look at it, Lana. I'm too big to take a virgin. Especially a tiny little thing like you."

I thought his description of me was ludicrous. I was thin, but saw myself as tall and gawky, by no means tiny. But I did kind of like *him* thinking of me that way.

Despite all of his protests, he was still working that wonderful finger into me, deeper and deeper, until he reached a barrier. He tested it, rather thoroughly, before he seemed to understand what it was. He cursed fluently, but didn't remove that thick finger. "That's your fucking hymen," he said, his eyelids heavy.

I leaned my breasts into his face, rubbing a hard nipple against those soft, mean lips. He took it into his mouth, sucking on it with a sexy groan. "Pleasure me, Akira. Please. I want you to make me come. You can do it with just your fingers and your mouth, right? Would that gross you out, to use your mouth on my pussy? Do you think it's ugly?"

He made a hot little noise of protest, his finger moving inside of me, working in and out of me in tiny little strokes. "No, baby, your pussy is so fucking pretty. I would love to get my mouth on you. It's the prettiest fucking thing I've ever seen."

I wanted to giggle at the ridiculous thing I'd gotten him to say, but my breath caught in my throat. I still loved to tease him, even while we were doing this.

I gripped his hair as he suckled at my breasts. "What about my breasts? Do you think my breasts are pretty?"

He moaned. "Baby, every inch of you is impossibly gorgeous, and I know you know it, you little minx."

"I don't know it unless you tell me, Akira. I've only ever cared what *you* think. I don't care about anybody else."

"Well, you're beautiful, Lana. Painfully so." He stroked me with that finger, bringing his other hand to my sex and rubbing circles on just the perfect little spot. *So that's my clit*, I thought as my gaze started to go fuzzy with the pleasure of it. His fingers were doing just the perfect things, and he brought me to the sweetest climax. I panted his name softly.

He had me on my back on the couch, his face buried between my legs before I even knew his intent. I nearly screamed in shock at the pleasure of it. He licked and sucked and used those wonderful hands to bring me to another mind-blowing orgasm.

After that, he worked on me slowly, kissing and licking and stroking all over my body, finally coming up to my mouth for a long kiss. I groaned as I tasted myself in his mouth. "I need you inside of me, Akira," I said, when he finally pulled back.

He shook his head, his mouth tight, his eyes pained. "I'm a bastard for doing this much, Lana. I don't deserve to lay even a finger on your perfect skin."

I reached down, gripping his impressive length and working him free of of his shorts. Our eyes were locked as I spoke. "I'm eighteen, and I'm determined that I don't want to be a virgin anymore. I went on the pill two months ago. Would you rather it be you to take my virginity, or do you want me to give it to some jerk I meet at college? Maybe I'll give it up at a frat party. Would you prefer that, or would you rather bury this beautiful cock inside of me tonight. I'll let you pick."

He groaned, and I knew instantly which option he'd chosen. He held my thighs wide apart with his hands, lining himself up at my entrance, his eyes intense and hungry. "Last chance to change your mind, Lana," he said on a gasp.

I reached down to stroke him, trying to tug him inside of me. He began to push in with a harsh groan. He worked himself in agonizingly slowly, inch by hard inch, feeding that magnificent length into me with his hand. He stopped when he'd reached that barrier. His breathing was ragged. "This is going to hurt. I'm sorry; it's unavoidable. I need to rip this barrier. It will only hurt like this the first time, okay?"

I just nodded, wanting him deeper inside of me, no matter the pain. He propped himself on both elbows above me, tensing his entire body in preparation. He thrust in hard, sinking to the hilt with the force. He shuddered as he paused inside of me, waiting for me to get used to the fullness. It had hurt a lot, but it still felt good, too. I was so achy and needy for him, and had wanted this for so long, that the pain seemed like a little thing when compared to the joy I felt at finally having him inside of me. He brought a hand between us, circling my clit with his thumb. I began to writhe.

"You're so fucking tight that I'm going to embarrass myself, baby. I want you with me when I come," he whispered. His sexy words, combined with all of the wonderful things he was doing to me, made me pant with my building orgasm.

He began to thrust, big, heavy thrusts that went on and on, his finger still working on me. He kept going until I began to clench around him with another glorious orgasm. "Yes," he grunted as he began to shudder and come himself. "Oh, yes, Lana."

After we'd recovered, he carried me up to his bed, tending to me and holding me. We spent the night together, and it was the best night of my life. He made love to me, over and over again, worshipping my body with his. The spell wasn't broken until morning, when he was thrusting inside of me yet again. He had used me so thoroughly that I was deliciously sore, each movement reminding me of how much he'd enjoyed my body. He brought me to climax first, before he let himself go.

"I love you, Akira," I said to him as he lay on top of me when we'd finished. My voice was quiet, but sure. "I always have, and I always will. I want to be with you forever. I don't want anyone else."

He stiffened at my words, immediately taking his weight off me and sitting up on the side of the bed, his back to me, his legs on the floor. "That's not possible, Lana," he said, his tone very final.

My heart stopped in my chest, my mind racing. "You said you and Milena had broken up," I said, my voice sounding accusatory.

He turned to look at me, his features anguished and severe. "We are. This has nothing to do with Milena. This has to do with you. You have the world at your feet. And you're still so young. You can't possibly know what you want, at your age. You need to go to college. You need to go experience life and see the world. You're unbearably beautiful, and smart, and your family's wealth means that the sky is the limit for you. You have an amazing life ahead of you, and I would never dream of being the thing that stood in your way. This can't be anything more than what it was, Lana. It was an incredible night, you were incredible, but I won't tie you to this rock. I'm not that selfish."

His tone was kind, even tender, but all I heard was a rejection. In just a few short minutes, he had stomped all of my dreams of a happy life into dust.

I was a little numb that morning as I showered, dressed, and left his house. He hovered over me, studying me with worried eyes as I prepared to leave.

"Are you okay, Lana?" he asked, his voice concerned. But he didn't touch me, not once. He didn't correct his clear rejection, or take it back. And he never even came close to saying that he loved me, too.

I left his house with a broken heart.

I galvanized myself into professing myself to him one more time, going to his bar that afternoon. I would hate myself if I didn't give it my best shot. I couldn't just give up on the thing that I'd always wanted.

I never even got a chance to speak to him again. I was told by the bartender that he was in his office. I went to the employees only section of the bar without asking. No one paid me any mind. They were all used to me doing as I pleased, since I had dogged Akira's every step for years now, going wherever I wanted whenever I pleased.

I nearly barged into his office before I heard the voices nearly shouting inside. The door was open just a crack, and I peeked inside. Milena was pressed against Akira, his hand in her hair. They were embracing, though they were talking, not kissing, as it at first appeared. It was still a clear embrace, though.

"Don't lie to me. I saw that little piece of jailbait leaving your house this morning! I'll *kill* her!" Milena was saying to him, her voice low and mean.

"Leave her alone, Milena. It isn't what it looked like. Lana is just a family friend with an inconvenient infatuation. Just leave her alone, k?" His voice was earnest and pleading.

I backed away from the doorway, my hand flying to my chest. *He's still involved with* Milena, I realized in horror. I had shamelessly seduced him, not taking no for an answer, but he hadn't wanted *me*. He was clearly concerned that he might lose the one that he really cared about, going by the earnest note in his voice. If he did lose her, it would be my fault. *He must hate me*, I realized, so disgusted with myself that I wanted to be sick. I was just a family friend with an inconvenient infatuation, he'd said. I walked away on leaden feet, feeling sick down to my soul.

I flew off the island that night. I didn't return for eight long, desolate years.

CHAPTER ELEVEN

PRESENT

The staff at the hospital recognized us both on sight. My family was well known on the island, and Akira was, well, Akira. He was a local legend. We got the local treatment, a nurse taking me back immediately and cleaning off my cuts in short order, Akira hovering at my back the entire time.

"She got you good," the nurse said as she checked over the cuts very carefully. She was a local, a short, heavy-set woman with a friendly face and a long black braid running down her back. "But it'll heal up in a few days. You don't need stitches or nothin'." She grinned suddenly. "Word is you won. Good job. Milena beat up my cousin a few months ago, and for no good reason. I hate that crazy bitch." Word traveled fast on the island, apparently.

I couldn't help it. I grinned back proudly. "I tried not to resort to fighting like a girl, but you gotta do what you gotta do." Akira tugged on a lock of my hair. It was a reprimand, I knew.

The woman threw back her head and laughed. "That's a good one."

We were in and out of the hospital within a half an hour, thanks to the local treatment. "Just be sure to avoid any sitting water, and the ocean of course, until those cuts close up good," the nurse instructed.

That killed my good mood. I had wanted so badly to go surfing again in the morning.

I was sullen as Akira pulled me by the hand out of the hospital and to his car.

"Can we go to your house?" I asked him as he pulled out of the parking lot. I was a little worried that he would drop me off at the resort.

He didn't look at me as he grimaced. "Tutu and Mari will torture me for at least a month if we don't swing back by the shops and show them that your arm got patched up fine."

"And then can we can go to your house?" I asked.

He sent me a searching look. "Yeah," he said.

I felt a wave of relief. I had been worried that, after the drama-filled night, he wouldn't want to spend any more time with me.

I considered what to do the next day, since we couldn't go in the ocean. I sighed heavily. "I guess I need to work all day tomorrow. Since I can't surf, and I'm already hopelessly behind on my schedule. I'll need to start really early, I suppose."

He glanced at me, his eyes almost sad. "Please, don't. Spend the day with me," he said. It was a simple request, uttered in his gentlest tone, and nothing on earth could have made me refuse him.

"I never could say no to you," I told him, revealing my vulnerability. It wasn't as though I'd ever been able to hide it.

He gave me a wicked grin at that. "I'll be taking advantage of that. You might regret telling me that."

I sighed, my chest hurting a little. "Never. I'd be happy if you wanted anything from me, anything at all. It's always been that way, Akira. You must know that there's nothing I wouldn't do just to make you smile."

"Oh, Lana," Akira said, stroking a hand over my hair, his eyes sorrowful. I wondered if he looked so sad because my heart was in my eyes, and in my voice, and he felt bad that he could never return those kinds of feelings, not for me.

We were silent for the last few minutes of the drive, both of us lost in our own thoughts.

He opened my door, holding out a hand to help me out. He had me pinned to the side of the car in a flash, his mouth on mine in a hard, passionate kiss. He didn't pull back for long minutes. I pressed up against him, snaking my arms around his back to squeeze his butt. He jumped a little, but didn't stop me, so I took full advantage, gripping him to me, and caressing that perfect butt at my leisure.

When he finally ended the kiss, I protested. He just kissed the top of my head, pulling me towards the bar.

"I've been dying to kiss you all afternoon," he told me.

I was both floored and thrilled by his words.

Only the bar remained open, so Mari and Tutu had taken up residence there, since their own establishments were closed for the night.

Mari started humming the theme to *Rocky* loudly when we walked in the door. Tutu joined in, showing the room her impressive shadow boxing techniques in accompaniment. Their little show of support had me laughing until tears ran down my face. They had the entire room joining in, even eliciting a rare, loud, carefree laugh from Akira.

Tutu and Mari were in such rare form that we ended up sitting at the bar and talking with them for four hours, catching up and joking and just talking like we used to. It was like old times, and I had missed old times.

Akira sat in a barstool beside his female relatives, but when I went to take the seat beside him, he'd just pulled me tight against him. I stayed in his arms for the joy-filled evening, soaking him in as I leaned against him, his arms tight around me. When it became clear that we weren't going anywhere anytime soon, he stood, tugging me into the chair, but resuming a similar hold on me from behind, but with him standing. He was affectionate and cuddly, stroking my hair, and bending down to kiss the top of my head often. His actions seemed to make Tutu and Mari giddy with excitement. They kept elbowing each other, huge smiles on their faces every time he kissed my head. He didn't seem to care what they had assumed by the way he was acting, so I didn't let it trouble me either. If he wanted to touch me, I wanted to be touched.

Tutu was well into her cups when she began to get truly outrageous. She pointed an accusatory finger at me.

"Are you on the pill?" she asked, her tone low and mean.

I nodded, laughing as she clutched at her heart, shuddering. "That will make you barren. It's a fact. Get off those pills immediately. It might already be too late. Let me see your purse."

Someone from the resort had delivered my red handbag, and I'd stashed it under the stool, but I shook my head.

The bag was at my feet, and she dove for it, bouncing back spryly when she had a good grip on it. I just laughed, wondering what she was doing. She dug through it, fishing out my packet of birth control pills almost immediately. My eyes widened. *What was she up to now?*

"Um, I need those, Tutu. What on earth are you doing?"

She shook her head stubbornly, pursed her lips, and took off for the bathroom, running like she was sixteen instead of sixty. I turned in Akira's arms, giving him a baffled look. "Akira, that was my birth control. This is bad."

He just shrugged, looking way too unconcerned about the whole thing. I got up with a sigh, intending to follow crazy Tutu.

Mari sent me a strange look, as though she thought *I* was crazy, and Akira pushed me back into the stool, wrapping those massive arms around me tightly. "You don't want to be alone with Tutu in a small space when she's in a mood like this, Lana. Trust me. The pills can be replaced."

I sighed, supposing he was right.

Tutu returned shortly, rubbing her hands together and cackling as she stepped out of the bathroom, the pills obviously absent.

"Has she gotten even crazier?" I asked her children, my tone idle.

They both just made noises of noncommittal.

"You can thank me later, since I'm feeling generous," was the first thing she said as she rejoined us.

I snorted loudly.

She rubbed her hands together. "Mari and I will plan the wedding. It will be outside, and the weather will be perfect." Her tone implied that she had some control over that.

I turned and gave Akira a pointed look. "You want to set her straight? Don't you think this is a bit much?" I asked him quietly.

He just shrugged, smirking. "Why bother? Let her have her fun."

I thought it might be time to leave, since the place had officially turned into crazy town. I told Mari as much.

She just gave me an arch look. "And how crazy are you, pretty girl, that you didn't know it's been crazy town all along?"

That made me laugh, and lightened the mood, the conversation, too.

I was shocked when I checked the time and saw that it was nearly two a.m. "How late do you guys normally stay up? It is way past my bedtime."

"Don't you know it's Friday night?" Tutu asked. "I won't leave until they kick me out."

Mari gave me a level stare. "She's not joking."

"Say goodnight to Lana. I'm taking her home," Akira said, hearing my comments. Both women protested, but hugged me goodbye.

"I'll set up a spa day for the day after tomorrow. Does that sound good?" I asked them. They both nodded enthusiastically.

I heard Tutu's last comment as we were walking out the door. "He's going to keep her in bed all day tomorrow." She had projected her voice loudly, as though telling the entire bar.

I was still laughing as Akira pulled me to his car.

CHAPTER TWELVE

He was serious on the drive to his house. "You need to be careful of Milena. It's hard to know what she's capable of. You got the better of her that time, but she is usually a better fighter than that. I've seen it. I think she was just so mad that she forgot how to fight. If you see her out in public, you need to *walk away*. I don't want you getting hurt. She'll have twice as much to prove now."

I shrugged. "I'll be gone soon enough. I doubt I'll run into her."

He gave me a hooded glance out of the corner of his eye, his gaze returning quickly to the road. "Are you so anxious to leave us again?" he asked, his voice very quiet.

I didn't answer, stewing for a while. I decided I didn't owe him an answer. Not for a question like that.

His hand went to the back of my head, gripping my hair tightly. I sent him a surprised glance, but his face was closed off, his eyes on the road as he pulled left onto the private drive that led to his house.

He started kissing me as soon as he opened my door, pushing me against the side of his car. He yanked up my skirt, lifting me against him. I wrapped my legs around his waist, and he groaned. It was a sound of approval from deep in his throat.

He used the weight of his hips to push me high against the car, and used both hands to pull the top of my dress down. He dragged his heavy arousal against me all the while, making me moan. We were in his driveway, in full view of his neighbors, if they cared to look, but I couldn't bring myself to care, not even a little. Even it if had been broad daylight out instead of two-thirty in the morning, I doubted I would have turned him down. I had always been his for the taking. Anytime, anywhere.

"You said you could never tell me no," he said roughly, unclasping the front closure of my bra.

My only response was a moan as he kneaded at the heavy globes. He shrugged out of his own dress shirt, ripping more buttons than he ended up unbuttoning in his hurry. He shifted me away from the car, melding our bare chests together.

"Did you mean it, when you said that?"

I felt his hand working below me, and then his bared erection was pressing against me. He shifted aside the tiny scrap of lace that served as his only barrier, poising himself at my entrance in a flash. He worked into me with his hands on my hips, my passage already slick enough to ease his progress. He buried himself to the hilt, but didn't begin to thrust right away, instead holding himself there, so impossibly deep inside of me.

He used both of his arms to hug me securely against him as he began to walk, moving to his front door now that he'd buried himself inside of me.

I was lost, each step sending excruciating waves of pleasure straight to my core. My thighs were wrapped tightly around his hips. When he used one hand to unlock his front door, I rubbed against him, dragging my nipples against his chest, my sex clenching him as I wiggled against him. He moaned, ramming into me hard with the same motion he used to shut the front door behind us. He pulled out of me with excruciating slowness, ramming back in much harder and faster, then pulling out slowly again, dragging his thick cock against all of the right spots.

"Faster, Akira, I want you to fuck me hard and fast," I told him on a ragged breath. I wanted to drive him crazy. It worked.

He grabbed my hips and rocked into me. He pounded me against the closed door like his life depended on it, my nails raking his back as I screamed his name. It was almost painful, with his huge girth, but I still loved it.

"*This* is paradise. You took my paradise with you when you left, Lana," he rasped into my ear. The words drove me over the edge, and I shouted his name as I came. He followed, burying his face into my neck as he shuddered against me.

He surprised me by biting my neck as the shudders eased. I yelped in surprise. "I'm going to wring so many orgasms out of you that you'll be too exhausted to even think about leaving this rock," he growled into my ear.

I laughed, feeling almost drunk from the aftershocks of the powerful orgasm. "You're welcome to try," I murmured back.

He pulled out of me slowly, making us both groan in the process. He shifted me around until I was cradled against his chest. His look was a warning. "Baby, I won't be trying. I'll be doing."

I made a contented little noise, burrowing my face into his chest. He stroked my hair, the tender gesture belying the mean look on his face.

He laid me on his bed, pulling my clothes off with swift, economical motions. I just lay where he left me, feeling a little boneless as he disappeared into his bathroom. I heard a bath running and a moment later, he was back striding towards me, completely nude. I drank in the sight of his perfect body as he moved.

I sighed a little dreamily. "You're magnificent," I told him. It was a fact.

He smirked at me, bending to pick me up. "Look who's talking," he said with a grunt, flipping me onto his shoulder. He squeezed my butt as he carried me into the bathroom. He was much gentler as he lowered me into the scorching hot water. He turned back to grab something on the counter, and I got a full, unencumbered view of his perky butt. I made an appreciative little, "Mmmmm," at the sight.

He threw a grin over his shoulder. "You always were obsessed with my butt. I couldn't go out in public without being stalked when you were in high school. You did love to talk about my ass. Do you have any idea how embarrassing it is for a grown man to get his ass ogled by high school girls every time he goes out in public?"

I laughed until tears streamed down my cheeks, because it wasn't an exaggeration, and I had simply adored tormenting him with my little schemes back then. The old memories warmed me. I had made a point to tell just about anyone who would listen just how unparalleled his ass was, and my high school friends had been paying attention. All of our eyes had followed Akira whenever we had been lucky enough to catch a glimpse of him coming or going.

He joined me in the steaming water, and we washed each other with lingering touches. I straddled him so I could wash his thick hair. He kissed me, and I could feel him growing hard against me.

I shifted, trying to work him inside of me, but he pulled back.

"I want you in bed," he told me, rising.

We dried off, and he tugged me to the bed, pushing me onto my back, and moving over me. He brought our faces close together.

He watched me, his expression almost wary. We stared at each other for a long time before he cupped my face in his big hands.

"Don't leave us again, Lana," he whispered roughly. "Don't leave *me*. Stay. Please."

I shook my head, not understanding, not even letting myself hope that he meant what I longed for him to. "Why, Akira?"

"Because I was wrong. I thought I was doing the right thing when I told you to leave the first time, but I was *so wrong*. I thought you'd see the world and that your infatuation with me would evaporate. I thought you were too young and inexperienced to see that. But you were right. I was the one that was blind. I loved you then. I adored the ground you walked on, and nothing has changed. I knew I wouldn't stop loving you, but I was wrong to doubt you, wrong to think that your feelings would change. I've been consoling myself for so long with the idea that even if I was miserable without you, at least you were happy out there somewhere. And now that I know that's not the case, I can't bear the thought of you leaving me again."

My heart twisted painfully in my chest. It was hard to imagine that something I had wanted for so long would just suddenly appear before me. It felt surreal, and I just stared at him dumbly for a few long moments.

"What about the things you said to Milena back then? About me being a family friend with an inconvenient infatuation? Why would you say that if it wasn't true?"

"It's the only way I could think of to manage her. We were broken up, and she was threatening to hurt you. I knew her threats weren't idle. I've seen her do some pretty awful things, and I couldn't think of another way to stop her from hurting you."

"I thought you'd forgotten me," he continued, "until some of your friends stopped by to see me. James and Bianca painted a different picture for me, and when I realized that you hadn't forgotten about me, I contacted your father. He didn't know that I intended to get you to stay when I talked him into getting you to come to Maui. In fact, I feel like a bastard for manipulating him, knowing that he probably won't be pleased to know that you and I are…"

I shook my head. Akira had never understood how highly my father regarded him. He was like another son to my father, but Akira had always been too blind to see it.

"I love you, Lana, and I want you to stay. You said you could never say no to me, and I intend to hold you to that. *Marry me.*"

He hadn't made it a question, as though he just couldn't quite do it, and that made me smile even through my tears.

He wiped the tears away as I nodded tremulously. "Yes," I said, my heart filling with joy. I hadn't been lying. I was literally incapable of telling him no.

He smiled, moving against me, and the relief in his face let me know just how much he'd feared my refusal.

"I love you," I said breathlessly, as he pushed himself inside of me.

"Good," he murmured roughly, "because I'm keeping you forever."

"I'm planning our wedding, not Tutu and Mari," I told him some time later.

He was folded against my back, his hand stroking my hip idly, while we caught up.

He kissed the side of my head. "It's cute that you think that. Let me know how it works out for you."

I laughed. "You don't think I can go toe to toe with your mother and win?"

"I don't think anyone can."

"We'll just see about that."

CHAPTER THIRTEEN

In the end, it was a compromise. Tutu wanted to plan the wedding in two weeks. I wanted two months. We settled on one. I wanted a smaller ceremony, with family and our closest friends. Tutu thought it was completely rude not to invite the entire island. She was closer to winning that one than I was, though I insisted on a ceremony on the beach at my family's villa, and I got my way there.

I made my dear friend Bianca fly in a week before the wedding. Since she'd retired from being a flight attendant to be a painter full-time, we'd taken to calling each other nearly every day. I'd been helping her plan her own wedding, and I thought that it was only fair that she become equally involved in my own special day.

James, her ridiculously possessive fiancé, couldn't join her for several days, and I picked her up myself from the airport for some one-on-one girl time. Well, as one-on-one as we could get, since she had a full-time bodyguard that tried to follow her everywhere. Considering that she'd been shot just a few months ago, I couldn't completely blame her crazy future husband for going to such lengths. Two men had died in the attack, and she, her bestie, and her bodyguard had all been shot. I had heard about the whole thing after the fact, when she was in the hospital. I thought of how worried I'd been when I heard about the tragic incident. They'd known she would live by the time I learned of the attack, but I'd rushed to her side, completely distraught. I couldn't even imagine how James must have felt.

We hugged. She tried to pull away first, but I held on tight. "Thank you so much for coming," I said into her good ear. "I know it must have been a fight. Is James still having a hard time letting you out of his sight?"

She laughed, and I pulled back to look at her. Her hair nearly covered the quarter-sized, pink scar back near her jaw. It still made me want to cry every time I saw it. Not because it looked that bad, but because I'd heard the story of how it had happened, and the thought that we had come so close to losing her was still a tender wound for me.

The scar got to me, but Bianca seemed completely over it. She didn't try to hide it, or show it off. It was as though she'd already forgotten about it. Even the hearing aid that she'd had to adopt didn't seem to affect her, and I'd only heard her complain one time about the fact that she hadn't been able to eat solid food for over a month after the attack.

I'd made a comment once about the fact that a traumatizing incident that would have defeated most people seemed to have barely affected her.

"We were so lucky that it's hard to sweat the small stuff anymore," she'd responded with her little shrug. She was just like that, weathering storms in that quiet way of hers. She fascinated and impressed me in so many ways, because she was both one of the most soft-spoken, and one of the strongest women that I'd ever met.

"Jackie tried to come with me," she told me, as we walked to my car. "I had to put my foot down. I wanted some time with just the two of us, but I guarantee she'll be here within two days."

I smiled. I could tell by her tone that Jackie was growing on her. "And how many days do you think James and Stephan will stay away?"

She pursed her lips, taking the question more seriously than I'd intended. "I predict they'll come together, and if they don't show up by tomorrow, I'll be surprised. I actually think that Stephan will be the one to egg James on, because James is afraid he's been too smothering since the attack, and Stephan would never think of it that way. The only girls' time we're guaranteed is today, most likely, so what should we do before my boys crash the party?"

I laughed at her matter-of-fact tone. She didn't sound a bit put-out about it, either, which was good, because I couldn't imagine James becoming less possessive of her time in the near or distant future.

"Well, we need to stop by for a last dress fitting. It shouldn't take too long, so how about an afternoon at the spa?"

"Sounds like a plan," she said easily.

We met Mari at the bridal shop. She was my maid-of-honor, and Bianca was a bridesmaid, but it was the first time the two of them had met. I was relieved but unsurprised when they got along right off the bat. Neither were the type to cause drama.

I tried on my short silk wedding dress, pleased with the fit. It was a simple design, and perfect for the beach. I couldn't have been happier with how it had turned out. It hugged my curves in a flattering way, showing my legs off to advantage.

Mari and Bianca tried on their light blue silk dresses. They were designed very similarly to my wedding dress, and both of the stunning women were suited to the look, if in very different ways.

"Have the other bridesmaids pay me a visit as soon as they get into town," the dressmaker told me as we left. The fitting hadn't taken more than a half an hour. "The sooner the better."

I nodded that I would. Sophia and Jackie weren't due in town for three more days, but I would pass the message along.

We spent a long, lazy afternoon at the spa, Mari joining us as we caught up on every little thing. Tutu showed up within an hour of our arrival, and Bianca and I good-naturedly gave up on a day of one-on-one time. There was plenty of time for that later, when we weren't in the midst of wedding madness.

I could tell right away that Tutu liked Bianca, but that she liked messing with her, too.

"You aren't another tall blonde woman that's here to steal our local men, are you?" Tutu asked Bianca with a glare, as we had our toes done. "Around here, we smack the nerve right out of white girls for doing that."

Bianca wasn't intimidated, as Tutu had been expecting. Instead, she threw her head back and laughed. She pointed at Tutu, still smiling. "I've heard all about you, Tutu. Lana warned me that you might call me a haole and give me a hard time. I'm ready for you. But you don't have to worry about me stealing any men. I'm engaged, and he's not a local, though when you get a look at him, you'll still probably want to smack me."

Tutu grinned back at her. "You're another sassy blonde girl. I like that."

I was relieved. When Tutu decided to dislike somebody, things got a little too interesting. I could only hope that she wouldn't take exception to any of my other bridesmaids.

Bianca was staying with me at my family estate, since it was the location of the wedding, and there was plenty of room for all of the mainland bridesmaids and groomsmen. Akira and I hadn't even considered the idea of sleeping separately until the wedding, so he was staying there with me, as well.

He met us the second we all came, laughing, through the front door of the villa. He was smiling. I quickly saw why as two men appeared behind him.

Stephan didn't hesitate, striding forward with a smile to embrace a startled Bianca, and then me. He politely introduced himself to Mari and Tutu while I glanced at James, who was still hanging back, studying Bianca with a wary look. I glanced at her.

She looked a little surprised, but not unhappy, that she'd been followed.

As though he couldn't help himself, James moved to her, crushing her against him as he said something into her ear that had her blushing profusely as he pulled back.

"And how are you, Lana?" James asked, looking towards me with a grin.

I grinned back, knowing the part he'd played in my own personal bliss. "As well as you could expect, considering that I have the best friends in the world."

Jackie and Camden, and Parker and Sophia all showed up two days later, my parents a day after that. Watching my father with Akira did something very good for my soul, especially with everything on the table as it now was.

My father greeted Akira before he even gave me, his favorite little girl, so much as a glance. I didn't feel slighted, and I wasn't the least bit worried about his approval. He, like me, had only ever seen the good in Akira.

The two men embraced, and I saw that my father said something into Akira's ear that had the huge man looking suspiciously watery eyed.

I hadn't heard my father's words, but I did hear Akira's clear, quiet response. "Thank you, sir. That means the world to me."

My dad was in his fifties, but still a very handsome man. Camden and I both took after our mother in looks, but I thought that we'd both have been fine taking after him, too. Our dad was tall and elegantly built, with silver hair and warm brown eyes that at that moment somehow reminded me of Akira. He had the warmest, most enchanting smile, and it enchanted me more than ever when he turned it on Akira.

"Call me Dad," I heard him say quietly to Akira, and I just about lost it. I had to fight not to burst into sappy tears, at the dumbfounded, grateful look on Akira's face.

I asked Akira later what my father had said into his ear. He clenched his jaw, and I could see that he had to struggle not to get choked up at just the memory.

"He told me, 'About damn time, son.' I didn't expect him to approve."

"I know," I told him, giving him a tight hug. "Which is silly. He thinks the world of you, you know. He always has."

"I don't feel worthy. Of either of you."

I squeezed him tighter. "Well, you're just going to have to get over that. We're all family now. All we can hope is that Tutu doesn't try to box my dad's ears at the wedding."

I wasn't *really* worried about that possibility, but if I *was* just a touch worried, I needn't have been. When Tutu and my father finally met again, face to face, they embraced for so long, whispering into each other's ears, that my ravishingly beautiful mother had begun to shoot them some rather disgruntled looks. That was ridiculous, of course, because when they pulled back I saw the tears in Tutu's eyes. After all these years, she had finally thanked him for all he had done to mentor her son. I could tell by the look on my dad's face that it had been worth the wait.

As Tutu had predicted, the day of the wedding dawned sunny and picture perfect, and she took full credit for it.

Tutu wore light blue to match the bridesmaids for pictures, and she fussed over me as I dressed for the beach ceremony. I couldn't help taunting her a little as she worked on straightening the lei around my neck, her lips pursed.

"I told you so, Tutu," I told her quietly, with a smug little grin. It felt smug, but a happy kind of smug.

Her eyes shot up to mine, one sassy brow shooting straight for the sky. "What do you mean by that?"

"I told you years ago that I would marry Akira, and you told me it would never happen."

She snorted. "Silly girl. This was all my idea, the whole time. I was using reverse psychology on you, and you fell for it. You're welcome."

I laughed so hard that I had to have my eye makeup redone.

We had a short ceremony on the beach at sunset, with less than a hundred guests in attendance. We watched each other as we said our vows. Akira's face was stoic, but I could see the strong emotion in his eyes, and I was certain that he could read the adoration in mine.

I'd spent a little time regretting all of the years we could have been together, if I had just been brave enough to come back sooner, or if he had just been bold enough to contact me, but I felt at peace even with that, as I looked with clarity at the good years ahead of us. I knew that we would never take each other for granted, or fail to appreciate what we had. Our time apart had been painful, but it had forever assured us of that.

Akira gave me the biggest grin as we were announced man and wife. He looked breathtaking, his hair pulled back to show off his starkly handsome face, dressed in white, with a maile lei draped over his strong shoulders.

We had only invited about one hundred close friends and family to the beach ceremony, but the reception/wild party was a whole different story. There was only a short list of people on the island that *weren't* invited. The family estate was opened up and equipped for a hell of a party.

In a completely uncharacteristic move for me, I made no attempts to be a good hostess. I didn't greet all the guests, and I didn't make the rounds to mingle, or to share my time. I left that to…whoever. I knew my mother, father, my devilish brother, Camden, or hell, even Jackie, could take over those duties. This was supposed to be my day, and so I took that literally, doing the only thing I wanted to do. Akira and I danced, for hours and hours. We completely monopolized each other, stopping occasionally to chat and catch up with friends and family, but my goal was to spend as much of the magical night in Akira's arms, and I thought I succeeded admirably.

We weren't the only love-struck couple I caught mooning over each other that night. James and Bianca did much the same, dancing and sharing positively indecent looks for most of the night.

The party lasted into the next day, and we were dancing barefoot on the beach, out of sight from our guests, as streaks of dawn light began to color the sky.

Music from the party drifted to us. We were far enough away that we only caught bits and pieces of it, barely enough to keep rhythm.

Akira sprawled out on the sand at my feet suddenly, smiling up at me, as happy and carefree as I'd ever seen him. "Have you heard of the Hawaiian custom of wedding night beach sex?"

I gave him a rueful smile. I was long past the days of falling for all of the local custom shenanigans. Generally, any sentence that began with, 'Have you heard of the Hawaiian custom?' ended with a prank.

"No, I haven't. And it's past the wedding night. I'd say it's officially morning now."

"That's what I meant. Wedding morning beach sex. It's a well-known fact in these parts that if you have wedding morning beach sex you'll both live to be a hundred, at least."

"Technically, yesterday was our wedding morning. Today is the next morning." I broke off, giggling, as he tickled me until I fell on top of him.

"I think you're missing my point," he told me with a grin, still tickling me mercilessly.

"What's your point?" I gasped, trying in vain to tickle him back.

"We need to make love on this beach right now if we want to grow really, really old together." He let up tickling my waist, burying his hands in my hair to kiss me. I was straddling him by the end of that long kiss.

I pulled back to smile into his eyes. "Well, as long as it's really, really old," I murmured, resealing my lips over his.

BOOKS BY R.K. LILLEY

THE LOVE IS WAR DUET
BREAKING HIM
BREAKING HER – COMING SOON

THE WILD SIDE SERIES
THE WILD SIDE
IRIS
DAIR

THE OTHER MAN
TYRANT – COMING SOON

THE UP IN THE AIR SERIES
IN FLIGHT
MILE HIGH
GROUNDED
MR. BEAUTIFUL

LANA (AN UP IN THE AIR COMPANION NOVELLA)
AUTHORITY – COMING SOON

THE TRISTAN & DANIKA SERIES
BAD THINGS
ROCK BOTTOM
LOVELY TRIGGER

THE HERETIC DAUGHTERS SERIES

BREATHING FIRE

CROSSING FIRE - COMING SOON

THE BISHOP BROTHERS SERIERS

BOSS - COMING SOON

Visit Rklilley.com to join my newsletter.

BAD THINGS

CHAPTER ONE

DANIKA

I had the strangest shiver of premonition rock my body the first time I heard Tristan's voice. I heard it from a room away, as he said something offhanded to my boss, Jerry, and still I knew somehow that he would change my life.

I had an unruly armful of clean laundry and four dogs crowding my legs in my boss's cramped laundry room, when I heard the front door open, two men chatting as they entered the house. I wasn't alarmed. It was a chaotic sort of house, with all sorts of people coming and going at all hours of the day, *and* I recognized the sound of Jerry's voice instantly.

The other man that spoke was a stranger, but his voice was deep and it sort of rumbled through the house until it reached me. I had an instant and positive reaction to it. I had mixed feelings about men in general, having a rather sordid past with them as a whole, *and* having recently gone through a nasty breakup with a real piece of work. My ex had been an out of work, pothead loser, and he hadn't been the first loser that I'd wasted my time on. Still, I knew right away that I adored the sound of that deep, masculine voice.

I dropped the pile of clothes into the clean laundry pile in the clean corner of the room. My laundry skills were negligible, to put it nicely. I worked for Jerry and his ex-wife Beverley, as a live in nanny/housekeeper/dog walker/pool girl/gardener/whatever they needed me to do. It was well understood that I pretty much sucked at the housekeeper part of that arrangement, but it seemed to work for us all. I'd been working for them for two years, and we were going strong. Beverley and Jerry, dysfunctional exes, and awesome co-parents that they were, had become my closest friends and two of my favorite people on the planet.

I was dressed like a slob in too short black cheer shorts and a washed out gray UNLV sweatshirt, my straight black hair pulled into a rough ponytail, and not wearing a scrap of makeup, but I went to meet the newcomer anyway. My four favorite animals on the planet dogged my steps as I padded down the hallway.

Jerry's back was to me as I turned the corner from the hallway and into the black, stone-lined entryway, the stranger facing me. I saw at a glance that the stranger was young, sexy as hell, and straight-up Trouble with a capital T.

I knew trouble when I saw it, it being a very old friend of mine. Trouble for me was this nasty little self-destructive streak that I'd never quite been able to shake. A theme song even played in my head when I felt the big T getting close. *Four Kicks* was that song, and it cranked up to full volume with my first glance at him.

He was tall, and built like a linebacker, both muscular and massive.

He wore a tight black T-shirt that showcased every starkly muscled inch of his chest. His tattooed arms were folded across his chest in a casually attentive stance, but his presence commanded the room.

His face was handsome, with clean, even features that were dominated by pale golden eyes. He had a straight slash of a nose, with a rounded tip that would have brought him from handsome to pretty boy if he wasn't so damned big, and full lips on a wide mouth that popped killer dimples at me as it hitched up playfully. Those dimples were pure big T. His pitch-black hair was cropped short, with dark stubble lining his jaw. His easy smile was playful, but still managed to be sinister. It was a heady combination for someone who was on a first name basis with the big T.

Jerry turned to see what the other man was smiling about. He was a middle-aged man, short and balding, with a slight build. *His* face was far from handsome, with close-set eyes and a big nose, but I thought he had one of the best smiles in the world.

"Danika," Jerry said with that world-class smile. "This is my buddy, Tristan. He's going to be crashing on the couch for a few days. He's… uh…between residences."

I mentally groaned. Bev was going to kill him. One glance at Tristan and I knew he wasn't just a buddy. Jerry had a spotty history with helping out what he always thought was the latest rising star. He had big dreams of managing the next big rock band, and he took those dreams to extremes. He and Bev were both technically attorneys, but she was the only lawyer in the house that you could call employed. Jerry was too busy collecting unsigned bands to practice law.

I gave Jerry a pointed look. "Bev is going to string you up. She said that if you brought home one more out-of-work musician, that she was going to kick you out, and then I would get upgraded to a bigger room."

He grimaced. "Now, now, don't go jumping to conclusions. Tristan has a job. Look, he's not even carrying a guitar."

I eyed Tristan up. "What's the job?"

Jerry answered for him, which let me know that he was full of it. "He's a club promoter."

I rolled my eyes. "Is that the best you can do? That's Vegas code for *unemployed*, Jerry. My pothead ex-boyfriend even calls himself a club promoter, and I don't think he ever even leaves his house. You need to think up something better before Bev gets home."

Tristan laughed, not looking even slightly offended by our exchange. "I *am* a club promoter, and I do also happen to be in a band," he said in a low, sexy drawl.

Oh lord, I thought, *Four Kicks* by Kings of Leon playing at full volume in my head as I heard his voice at close range. And I tried to pretend that I hadn't even heard that sexy as hell laugh. I knew that we were going to be a dangerous combination. Bad things were going to happen if we spent too much time around each other.

"Don't let Bev hear you say that," I warned him. I was really just trying to help Jerry out. I didn't want him to get into trouble with Bev again, and he never seemed to have a clue just what would set her off, even though it was always very obvious to me.

I sighed, knowing that this wouldn't be easy to fix. I tensed as I heard the loud garage door opening across the house. Bev's house was a huge, rambling, ranch style house, but the garage door was so loud that it always announced her presence.

I gave Jerry a stern look, sometimes feeling like his mother, even though he was forty-five, and I was barely twenty-one. I pointed at him. "I know what we need to do, but you're going to owe me. I hate lying to Bev." It was true. I was nowhere near nonchalant about the deception

I was about to undergo, and I wanted him to know it. Beverley was my hero. No one had ever helped me as much, or been as supportive of me, as she had. Plus, I just liked her. She was my closest friend, and I'd developed a serious case of hero worship for the successful, forty-eight year old woman.

"Tristan is a friend of *mine*," I told them. "Do not mention the words club promoter, or band. He is a plain old out of work student, and crashing for *one week* on the couch. We met at UNLV last semester. Got it?"

Jerry nodded, giving me a grateful smile. "You're the best, Danika. I owe you."

He sure did. I looked at Tristan, who was giving me that playful smile of his, as though we hadn't just barely met.

"You're a sassy little thing. I like that," he murmured, just as Bev and her boys rounded the corner that led from the garage and into the main living area.

Ivan and Mat caught sight of me and the dogs swarming at my heels and rushed me with huge whoops. Ivan was an unabashedly diabolical eight-year-old, and Mat was a precocious six-year-old, and the two of them combined were more than a handful, but I loved them to *pieces*.

Mat went straight for a tackle to my midsection, while Ivan caught the biggest dog, Mango, in a bear hug. Mango was a tan-colored bloodhound. She was nine years old and left a trail of slobber in her wake. She was a terrible guard dog. We were all convinced that if the place got robbed she'd just see it as an opportunity to lick more faces.

Mat squeezed my waist so hard that he drew a little grunt out of me. The second biggest dog, Dot, took exception to the rough handling. He growled menacingly at the six-year old. He was a big black Belgian

Shepherd, and none of us had any doubts that he was a good guard dog. A little too good, in fact. He'd taken to being my own personal protector, even against the other inhabitants of the house, and that included the boys.

I shushed Dot, hugging Mat back. He was a skinny blond kid with gorgeous blue eyes.

"You said you'd make us cookies when we got back!" Mat told me excitedly.

I nodded. "Okay. You gonna help me make them, or you want to go play while I cook?"

"Play!" he shouted. I didn't know if it was Mat, or being six, but the boy had a serious volume control issue. It just made me laugh.

"Okay. I bet you'll be able to smell them when they're done."

"Yes!" he shouted, even louder, then took off for his room.

Ivan straightened, looking around at all of the adults and pursing his lips. He had light brown hair, was tall for his age, and had soft brown eyes like his dad. He was a funny kid. He had moments of being a shameless brat, but just as many moments of absolute charm. "I want to play, too, Danika, but I'll help you if you really, really need me to."

I smiled at him. "I got it covered, buddy. You go on and play."

He took off, never saying a word to his dad or to Tristan. Typical eight-year-old, only paying attention to the one making cookies.

Beverley and I shared a look. She gave her boys a laughing eye roll before heading the same way they'd gone, towards her bedroom. She'd barely spared Tristan a glance. It wasn't a good sign.

"Jerry, a word," she called out, still moving towards her room. It didn't bode well.

He swore under his breath, but followed her.

I headed towards the kitchen. I felt Tristan following me.

The house was set up with an open floor plan. It was huge, but the entryway, living room, dining room, kitchen, and family room all shared one massive space, so it was a straight shot into the kitchen once I got around the giant L-shaped sofa that dominated the living room.

The house was a strange combination of shabby chic, leaning way further in the direction of shabby. Beverley was very successful as a worker's compensation attorney, and she came from a rich family, so money wasn't the issue when it came to the house. It was colossal, and in one of the nicest gated communities in Vegas, but the house was lined with outdoor carpeting and the furniture was in desperate need of an update. The only saving grace in the house was the spectacular artwork that she collected. Words couldn't even express how much I appreciated her fine eye for upcoming artists, but they were the *only* saving grace when it came to the house's aesthetics.

I understood why she didn't update a lot of it. New carpet would be ruined in just a few weeks by her unruly dogs and crazy kids, and the dark green leather sofa had the entire back gnawed off. I couldn't imagine a new sofa wouldn't receive the same treatment.

I had to unlock the the latch that had been installed on the side of the refrigerator before I opened it. Mango liked to eat sticks of butter when it wasn't latched tight...

I pulled out a plastic tube that was filled with chocolate chip cookie dough. I heard a clear, disappointed groan behind me.

I turned to look at Tristan, arching a brow at him. "What? You don't like chocolate chip?"

He shook his head at me, still showing off one dangerous dimple in a half smile. I really wished he'd put those dimples away. They were counter-productive to my peace of mind.

"You're joking, right?" he asked pointedly.

I had no idea what he was talking about. "Um, about what?"

"Cookie dough out of a plastic tube? Pre-made?"

I shrugged. "It's easy and fast, and they taste fine."

He shook his head again. "Show me to your baking supplies. I can't stand by and watch this."

I scowled at him. "You're bossy for an out-of-work houseguest," I told him.

"I have a job. Several actually. But yeah, I'm bossy. Show me to your flour."

I kept scowling, but I was walking from the kitchen and into the walk-in pantry while I did it. I waved a hand at the area that kind of held the baking supplies. The pantry was hardly well-organized, so he would probably have to dig around to get everything he needed for cookies.

I left him to it, going back into the kitchen to pre-heat the oven and grease a cookie sheet. I put out a large mixing bowl, measuring cups, and any other incidentals I thought he might need for baking. It was the least I could do if he was actually going to do the cooking.

I shrugged out of my sweatshirt, suddenly warm. It was a hundred and ten degrees outside, but you wouldn't know it by the way I normally froze inside of the A/C'd to death house. It wasn't normal for me to get so warm inside for no reason at all...

I was wearing a thin white tank and sitting on the counter when Tristan strolled back into the kitchen, his arms full of baking supplies.

He set them on the counter near the mixing bowl, lining them up neatly. His biceps bulged with the smallest movement. It was fascinating.

"Salt?" he asked me, his brow raised.

I blinked, trying to hear what he'd said. I pointed behind me after a few awkward moments.

He moved towards me without a word, and I saw my folly then. The cupboard I'd pointed to was directly behind me. I should have just grabbed it for him...

He didn't seem to mind, moving uncomfortably close to me to reach behind me. His upper chest got so close to my face that I could smell him. He smelled divine, so divine that I closed my eyes for a second to take it in.

He had to reach up, so his hip grazed my inner thigh as he shamelessly moved between my legs to get closer.

I gasped.

"Sorry," he said, backing up, the salt in his hand. I saw his eyes flick briefly down my body before he turned away, setting the salt beside the other ingredients.

"So you're the nanny, huh? You are *not* what I pictured when Jerry said he had a live-in nanny."

I glared at his back. "What did you picture?"

"I don't really know. I didn't have a clear picture in my head. I just wasn't expecting someone like you." He turned his head to flick me another unreadable glance.

I gave him a very unfriendly look, offended, and a little wounded. "What is that supposed to mean?"

"Nothing bad. Quit giving me evil eyes. Nannies just don't usually look like you. You're like what Hollywood would cast to be a nanny to add sex appeal to a movie. You're sexy. Really sexy. Don't play coy. You know you're gorgeous."

I stopped glaring, but I was wary of the compliments.

"Relax, okay?" he said, studying my face. "I'm not hitting on you, and I won't. What are you, like eighteen? Way too young for me. I'm just stating facts. Normally women don't appreciate other women as hot as you underfoot."

I was glaring again. "I'm twenty-one, and Bev is my best friend. I've been working for them for two years."

He threw up his hands, giving me an apologetic smile. "Sorry. I'm not trying to be a dick. It just surprised me that you were the nanny Jerry was telling me about. He gave me no hints that you were, well, hot."

"How old are *you?*" I asked him, still smarting from the too young comment.

"Twenty-six."

"That's not that old," I told him.

"I know. Just too young to be dating eighteen year olds, or even twenty-one year olds. Frankly, though, I'm bad with women my own age, too, when it comes to relationships, which is why I don't do them."

I couldn't help it. I had to ask. "So what do you do?"

"Hookups. Brief, casual hookups. How about you?"

I shook my head at him, pursing my lips at him. I couldn't quite believe that we had jumped to this already. He was a scoundrel, to be sure. "I do relationships. No exceptions. Never had a casual hookup in my life."

He sighed, measuring some flour into the mixing bowl. "Well, I guess that makes things less complicated. We'll be friends, then." He shot me a sidelong smile that was downright irresistible. I thought that this was one of the strangest conversations I'd ever had, being that we had just met. Only, it didn't feel like we'd just met. He spoke to me like he'd known me forever, and it was hard to refuse anything he said in that low voice of his.

I nodded, giving him my own, rather begrudging smile. "Okay, friends, since we'll be living under the same roof for the next week."

"Okay, then. My first job as your friend will be to show how to make the best damn chocolate chip cookies in the world."